Praise fo

"I got hooked on Christine go. ____ ___ _____. That was a cool way to make it happen. Nicely done."

"Suspenseful with Michigan history-I wanted to read before purchasing for my grandson and I enjoyed it, so I know he will. I have brought him books in the past but generally he had already read them and I know he will not have read this! Clever story, using Michigan history and very entertaining! This author is truly talented!"

"Great Purchase!. I love this author. Her books are very well written. ☺"

"Great new author-Loved this book! Already bought the first book of the other series. Worst part of the book was forcing myself not to peek at the end with each new twist or mystery in the story."

"The students loved the book! They came in each day with a question about what might happen. They made predictions about who the traitor was, and all but two students were surprised. The students and I learned a lot about the history of the 1770's. Your characters were interesting and we loved that some of them were based on true characters. All of the students want you to write more about these characters. Great job!"

"I enjoyed the story, the setting, and the action."

"I had trouble putting the book down. Couldn't wait to find out what was going to happen next. I look forward to reading more about the other characters."

"Can't put it down.-Get into your comfy chair. You'll be there for a while. This book is hard to put down."

Other Books by Marie LaPres

The Turner Daughters Series

Though War Shall Rise Against Me: A Gettysburg Story

Be Strong and Steadfast: A Fredericksburg Story

A Future of Hope: A Vicksburg Story

Forward to What Lies Ahead: A Petersburg Story

Wherever You Go: A Turner Daughter Prequel Novella

Other Titles

Whom Should I Fear?

Wisdom and Humility

Beyond the Fort Series

Beyond the Island

Beyond the Fort is dedicated to all historic interpreters. Thank you for keeping history alive.

First Paperback version August 2018

ISBN: 978-1981893270

Scripture quotations are from the New American Bible Revised Edition

This is a work of historical fiction; the appearance of historical figures is necessary. All other characters, however, are the product of the author's imagination and research, and any resemblance to actual persons, living or dead, is coincidental.

Cover Picture by Susan Emelander

Beyond The Fort

The Key to Mackinac
Book 1

Marie LaPres

DEMONSTRATION SITES AND PLACES OF INTEREST

*Alternate program or entrance available. Please see the *Guide to Access* for information.

#	
1	Native American Encampment
2	Cannon Platform
	▣ Firing Demonstration
3	Voyageur Landing
4	Water Gate
5	King's Storehouse
6	Guardhouse
7	Northwest Rowhouse
	▣ British Trader's House
	▣ Exhibit exit
	▣ British Trader's House, *Treasures from the Sand* exhibit entrance*

#	
8	Priest's House*
9	Blacksmith Shop
10	Church of Ste. Ann
11	Southwest Rowho
	▣ Merchant's Hou
	▣ Soldier's House
	▣ Trader's House
12	Bread Oven
13	Soldiers' Barracks
	▣ Redcoats on the

Michilimackinac

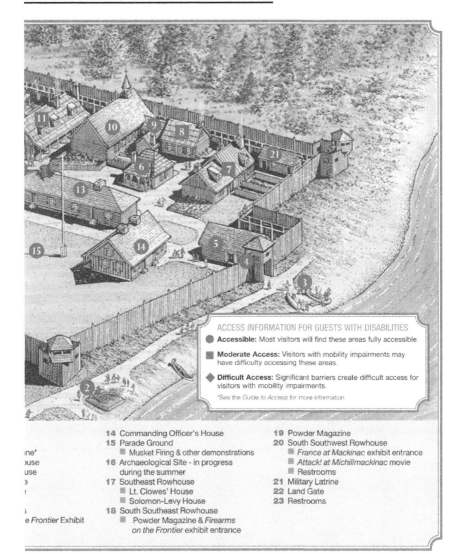

ACCESS INFORMATION FOR GUESTS WITH DISABILITIES

● **Accessible:** Most visitors will find these areas fully accessible.

■ **Moderate Access:** Visitors with mobility impairments may have difficulty accessing these areas.

◆ **Difficult Access:** Significant barriers create difficult access for visitors with mobility impairments.

*See the Guide to Access for more information.

ne*
ouse
use
e
!

s
e Frontier Exhibit

14 Commanding Officer's House
15 Parade Ground
    ■ Musket Firing & other demonstrations
16 Archaeological Site - in progress
    during the summer
17 Southeast Rowhouse
    ■ Lt. Clowes' House
    ■ Solomon-Levy House
18 South Southeast Rowhouse
    ■ Powder Magazine & *Firearms
    on the Frontier* exhibit entrance

19 Powder Magazine
20 South Southwest Rowhouse
    ■ *France at Mackinac* exhibit entrance
    ■ *Attack! at Michilimackinac* movie
    ■ Restrooms
21 Military Latrine
22 Land Gate
23 Restrooms

CHARACTERS

Christine Belanger: The heroine, a 16 year old girl working part time for the Mackinac State Historic Parks in Northern Michigan the summer before her Junior year of high school at Mackinaw City High School.

Henry "Henri" Beckwith: The hero, a 17 year old boy who snuck into Colonial Michilimackinac three years ago and passed through the portal into the past.

Mark Beckwith: Henry's brother, who went back in time with him.

Jacques Evans: Had once worked at Colonial Michilimackinac, found the portal and has been in the 1700's for over a decade. He now works as a fur trader and is considered a raconteur, or special tale-teller among the French community. He is also married and has three step-children.

Aimée Evans: An Ojibwa widow who is now married to Jacques. She has three children who are considered métis (half-French, half-American Indian)

Cort Lefevre: Aimée's son from her first marriage, he is in his early 20's. He is very stoic and serious as well as distrustful of newcomers. He has one son, Remy, and his wife is no longer in the community.

Simone Lefevre: Aimée's daughter from her first marriage, she is around the age of 18. She becomes fast friends with Christine.

Antoine Lefevre: Aimée's son from her first marriage, he is around the age of 13.

Raphael Lafontaine: Henry's best friend in Michilimackinac, he is around the age of 16. He is a voyageur who is fun-loving and usually happy. Aimee's nephew.

Callum Lewis: A British soldier who hates the French and does whatever he can to make their lives miserable.

Remington Hugo: A British soldier and Callum Lewis's second-in-command; he does a lot of the "dirty work".

Logan McIntosh: A British soldier.

A.S. DePeyster: British Commander of Fort Michilimackinac.

Rebecca DePeyster: Wife of A.S. DePeyster.

Sadie Morrison: Christine's friend and teammate from the present.

Rachel: Christine's oldest sister, also a teacher at Christine's school and her basketball coach, is married to Caleb Anderson.

Sean: Christine's brother, a lawyer who lives in Cheboygan.

Rebecca: Christine's sister, an accountant in Gaylord.

Anna: Christine's sister, a family practitioner in Petoskey.

Andrew: Christine's college-aged brother, getting a degree in Computer Sciences.

CHAPTER ONE

"Christine!" I took one more dribble, pulled up and shot the basketball with a flick of my wrist, smiling the moment it rolled off my fingers. It swished through the net, not even touching the rim. I turned and looked at my friend and teammate, Sadie Morrison, as she jogged across the gym towards me. She hadn't pulled back her long blonde hair yet, but had put on her blue basketball shorts and practice jersey.

"What's up?" I asked as I looked at the clock on the gym wall. I only had a few minutes left until I had to leave the gym and change for work. It was only the summer before my junior year of high school, but I needed a job to save up for college. Luckily, I lived in Mackinaw City, Michigan, one of the best tourist destinations in the Midwest. I had applied to work at one of the historical sites the day I turned sixteen and got the position.

"You need to shoot more three-pointers this year," Sadie said. "I still don't understand why you didn't last season."

"I just get nervous," I replied. "I don't want to miss and let the team down."

"We've got good rebounders, just in case you do miss. You have to work on your confidence, Christine." Sadie is my best friend, and one of the reasons for that was the fact that she is always a positive force in my life. I wish I had half as much confidence in myself as she did in me.

Sadie grabbed my rebound and flipped me the ball. "You're here early. Does that mean you have to work today?"

"Yeah. Coach understands, of course. She knows I'll put in the work on my own."

"I would hope Coach understands." Sadie gave me a smile. I knew what she meant. Coach better understand my situation because she was my older sister, Rachel. We have two other sisters and two brothers in between us. I hated being the youngest, always looked at as a child. That transferred over to work as well. Most of the employees of Mackinac State Historic Parks were college students. I got along well with them though, because I was so used to being around older people. I took one dribble, then shot another three-pointer. It swished through the net.

"I was just about to head in to shower quickly, then walk over to the fort." I didn't have a car yet, which I hated, but at least everywhere I went was pretty much within walking or biking distance.

"Well, we were going to head over to Second Beach later this afternoon. You should come when you're done with work." Second Beach was one of the best kept secrets in Mackinaw City. Few tourists knew about it, so it was a great local hangout.

"Will Dylan be there?" I asked hesitantly. Dylan Rodriguez was a boy that I had sort-of been dating, but he had simply stopped talking to me midway through April and was now spending time with Brittany Adams, a girl in our grade who tended to treat others as if they were beneath her.

"He might be there, yeah. But he's not worth you worrying, nor staying away from all the fun, Christine. You should still come."

"I might. I have an after-hours event I have to help with at the fort. We're teaching some people how to cook as a Colonial." I was excited. I love everything about history, which meant being a historic interpreter at a park like Colonial Michilimackinac was a dream summer job for me. Most of my friends didn't understand my love of history. There were many times when I felt as though I had been born in the wrong century. It was no surprise to anyone that I wanted to get my degree in history after high school.

Another benefit of working at the fort was getting to know people who liked history as much as I did.

"Well, come by after work, if you have time. As long as Old Man Evans doesn't get you. It's around that time of year, isn't it?"

I rolled my eyes as I faked a shot, dribbled and drove to the basket for a lay-up. I grabbed the ball and passed it to Sadie. "That is just a legend. There is absolutely no truth to it."

The legend of Old Man Evans had been around for as long as I could remember. Roughly ten years ago, one of the fort's employees, an older gentleman, almost 40 years old, by the name of Jack Evans had gone missing after work one day, never to be found. Many people had forgotten the story until three years ago, when two brothers from Mackinac Island had disappeared as well. They had told friends they were going to canoe across the straits and sneak into the fort for some mischief, but no one knew if they ever made it to the mainland. Their empty canoe was found near McGulpin Point but their bodies never surfaced. Some superstitious people claimed that Old Man Evans had gotten them, as they all had vanished around the same time of the year.

"Tell that to Mr. and Mrs. Beckwith. Their sons may still be out there." Sadie snapped back.

"Henry and Mark Beckwith probably drowned. There is no evidence of anything else happening."

"Unless, it's supernatural..." Sadie passed me the ball, then wiggled her fingers. "You know there are many French tales of ghosts and werewolves and..."

"Yes, Sadie." I shot the ball again, it banked off the backboard and fell into the basket. "But it is the end of June, not October. Fort Fright isn't for months."

"Yes, June. When Old Man Evans came and took the Beckwith Boys."

I looked at the clock, then held my hands out for one more pass from Sadie. She tossed the ball to me and I shot. "I'll see if I can get out to the beach tonight, I promise."

"Good." Sadie grabbed my missed shot and banked it in. "We miss you. It seems as though you're always at the fort."

"It's my job." I shrugged. Sadie should understand, as she had to help her parents run a local souvenir shop. Lucky for her, she was able to keep a more flexible schedule.

"All right." She dribbled behind her back. "I'll see you later tonight, hopefully."

"If not, I will see you at the scrimmage tomorrow." I nodded, then jogged towards the locker rooms to get ready for work. After I showered and was about to leave the locker room, I saw my sister, Rachel, the sister that is also my coach, lacing up her shoes in the coach's office.

"Christine!" She waved me over. "How was everything this morning?"

"It was good." I handed her the keys she had given me to get into the school that morning. That was another benefit of having a sister as your coach.

"Thank you," she smiled. "Hey, I need to tell you something. Caleb wanted to wait and tell the whole family on Sunday, but I feel compelled to tell you now." Caleb was Rachel's husband and was also the baseball and football coach for the high school. "I'm pregnant again. Due to have the baby in early November."

"Congratulations!" I hugged her, so excited at the prospect of another niece or nephew. "I cannot wait! Though the timing is not the best. That's right before our season starts."

"Yes, I know. We'll work that all out when the time comes. Mom and Dad are always willing to help, and that's the one season Caleb isn't coaching full-time."

"I am so glad you told me." I smiled, then checked my phone. "But I do have to get going or I'll be late for work."

"Of course, thanks for coming in early." I hugged her again, then headed into the dim hallway.

Just as I reached the outside doorway, I heard a few boys talking, and was going to ignore them when I heard my own name.

"Christine Belanger is pretty, I guess, but she's too much of a 'good girl' for me to date her," one of them said. I recognized the voice as one of my classmates'.

"Don't I know it. I spent a month and a half dating her and couldn't even get more than a kiss from her." That voice I knew right away, Dylan Rodriguez, my former boyfriend. One of the best-looking guys in the school, with shaggy, dark blonde hair, a swarthy complexion, striking blue eyes and a killer smile.

"Yeah, why did you ever date her?" A third voice asked. I strained to hear the answer, as I had wondered the exact thing when he first asked me out.

4

"I figured the connection would help me make varsity baseball. With Coach A. being married to her sister and all."

"Ha, that was brilliant, and it worked."

My heart fell. I knew I wasn't good enough for a guy like Dylan. He was funny, popular, and gorgeous.

"Yeah, and honestly, I'll probably hook back up with her in the fall, before basketball. Try and get a leg up on getting the starting shooting guard spot," Dylan replied.

"What makes you think she'll go back with you?"

"Because I'm me. What girl wouldn't? And it's not like the other guys are lining up to date her." Dylan's words hurt and his arrogance irritated me, but what upset me the most was that, had I not heard this conversation, he likely would have been right about me taking him back.

Once I made it to the Guide Shack at the fort, where all of the employees get ready for the day, take our breaks and keep many of our supplies, I threw on my skirt, shirtwaist and tied my apron string around my waist. I grabbed my cap and adjusted it. With a quick bend, I lifted my skirt up and tightened my sock garter, then arranged my clean basketball shorts underneath my colonial skirts. It was not quite historically accurate to wear, but no one ever noticed. I loved dressing in period clothes, it was one of my favorite parts of the job, but I was also quite thankful for my modern undergarments.

"Ready for the day?" I turned to see Marie, one of my co-workers.

"I've been up for hours," I answered. "Had to get a basketball workout in. Scrimmage tomorrow, then a softball game in the evening. That's why I'm off tomorrow." My summers were busy, but I wouldn't want it any other way.

"Gotcha. Who's scheduled for what today?"

I looked at the schedule. "It says that you are marrying Robert. Samuel is the priest. Alex and Nick are redcoats and Jem is the Fur Trader."

"Nice! I love a full staff, and marrying Robert." Marie smiled. I knew how she felt. Robert Reynolds was the fort's best-looking employee. With long blonde hair that was usually pulled back in a ponytail and light green eyes, as well as a perfectly muscled body. All of the female employees wanted to marry him in real life, not just at the reenactment. It was too bad he was seven years older than me, and good friends with my brother, Andrew.

"Who doesn't like marrying Robert? He is so cute!" I replied.

"Absolutely!" Marie exclaimed, her blue eyes shining. It was difficult not to like this young woman. Even though she was drop-dead gorgeous and looked like a "mean girl", she was always happy, nice, and looking for the best in people. It could be very frustrating at times, but it was impossible to hate her. "You look beautiful today!" She was complimentary as always.

"Yeah? Thanks." I never quite knew how to take compliments like that, especially standing next to the blonde beauty whose legs went on forever and whose figure was perfect even without stays. I just knew she was the prom queen down in Indiana, where she was from, and could have dated any guy she wanted.

I had more of an athletic build, strong, and solid. The boyfriends I had were mostly short-lived, and then there was the whole Dylan Rodriguez thing. Guys either thought of me as more like a friend, were jerks, or were intimidated by my older brothers. It's not as though I had many boys to choose from in our small school anyways.

I looked in the mirror and saw my dull brown hair, never staying in place. Marie's hair looked like a supermodel's, probably even right out of bed. I desperately needed the stays; when I didn't have them, I looked horribly frumpy. Marie probably never had a frumpy day in her life. Did she even know what frumpy was?

"No, really, Christine," Marie insisted. "Especially with that brown shortgown. You look great."

"Thanks, but standing next to you, I will always just be plain. I should actually just portray your servant."

"Oh, don't be silly." We began walking towards our assigned positions to prepare for the day.

"Hello, ladies." Jeremy Banks, also known as Jem, poked his head out of the Alexis Sejourne house. "How is everyone today?" He smiled at Marie.

"Very well, thank you!" Marie said.

"Very good." Jem was a nice guy, going into his senior year at Northern Michigan University. "Marie, are you excited for tonight?"

"What's tonight?" I asked, hoping I wasn't missing anything important. I knew Marie and I were doing a Colonial Cooking Class, but that wasn't anything that she would get excited about.

"A bunch of us are going to dinner in Indian River." Jem replied. "College night at the Brown Trout."

"Ah," I replied. The Brown Trout was a bar in nearby Indian River. There was no way I would be able to get in there as a sixteen-year-old.

"I wish we could get you in, Christine," Marie said.

"No worries," I replied. "Some of my friends are going to the beach tonight anyways. I won't be sitting at home alone." *Unless I want to.* I thought.

"Hey! Guys!"

We all turned to see the day's priest, Samuel Roddick jogging toward us. Samuel was kind of a local. His family owned a vacation home on Lake Michigan, and he had been coming up to Mackinaw City during the summer for years. He had just graduated from Michigan State University and was going to grad school for Historic Preservation at Clemson University. He was probably my favorite person to work with. "Look what I found!" He held up a very old-looking key.

"Ooohh. Very nice." Marie said, holding out her hand. "Where did you find it?"

"In the priest's garden. It never gets any attention, so I was hoeing in there and suddenly, it turned up."

"It looks like it could be a real artifact." I said.

"I wonder what it goes to," Jem added.

"Me too, I want to look around to find out." Samuel flipped the key in his hand. "But I have a full schedule this morning."

"So do I," Jem said, frowning.

"I'm cooking today," Marie shrugged, "so I won't be able to get away."

"I am just in the Piquet house doing crafts, so I should be able to find out what it goes to," I smiled.

"Make sure you're careful," Samuel tossed me the key. "Can't have the fort's little sister getting hurt."

I caught the key easily, though it was a bad throw.

"Aww, you get to have all the fun." Jem said playfully.

I didn't want to have them upset with me. "Well, I suppose I can wait and we can all look later." I slipped the key in my pocket, though I really wanted to do some exploring on my own. Maybe if I could discover something important, I could shake the "Fort's Little Sister" title off me.

"Sounds like a plan." Marie said, and we all parted and went to our assigned stations.

I didn't think about the key Samuel had found until later that night. I was all by myself, as I had volunteered to clean up after the cooking class on my own so that Marie could get ready for 'Brown Trout Night'. I was in no hurry to get to the beach to see my friends after hearing the boys tease Dylan about dating me. I took the key out of my pocket and held it up, looking at it closely.

"I wonder what it goes to." It looked old enough to be an actual key from the 18th Century, like the artifacts displayed in the Treasures in the Sand exhibit in the fort. There were very few structures that were original to the fort. "It was found in the priest's garden." I thought out loud, then I got one of my brilliantly random ideas. Quickly tightening the ties on my historically-accurate clothing, I grabbed my phone and power stick, then ran as quickly as my shoes could take me to the priest's house. When I got there, I glanced around to make sure no one else was present, then hopped over the plastic and wooden barrier. The root cellar in the priest's house was one of the only original sites still intact from the 1780 demolition. I found a small old ladder and lowered it into the cellar, then climbed down and looked around. I had never learned why this particular structure hadn't been excavated yet, but I was glad that it hadn't. I walked around the cellar, studying the walls. Nothing seemed out of the ordinary. I was about to climb back up the ladder when I tripped on a rock sticking out, then fell to the ground.

"Oww..." I looked down at my scraped hands. "Well, wouldn't it be nice for me to get through just one day without hurting myself. Never mind that." I turned and glared at the stone that had tripped me.

"Stupid rock." I stood and kicked at it, then bent to examine it closer. It was not a rock, but a ring of metal. The dirt had been hiding it, but had loosened when I tripped and then kicked at it. My stomach jumped as a flurry of excitement ran through me. I knelt, wanting to see what lay beneath. I knew that I shouldn't. Sara and the other archaeologists should examine it first, but I was too impatient. I scraped away the dirt, then pulled the ring hard several times before a trapdoor came open.

"Holy cow." I said, then pulled out the flashlight app on my phone to look below. There was a small, dirt-packed room, with an old rickety ladder leading down. This ladder seemed to be older, almost 'of the period'. My heart pounded as I carefully turned and put a foot on the first rung, praying that it wouldn't break.

"The archaeologists will kill me for this," I said to myself, but continued down the ladder anyway. When I got to the middle rung, it snapped, and I fell to the floor with a thud, dropping my phone. The trapdoor slammed shut above me. I quickly found my phone and dusted myself off. "Well, this is not my day," I looked around. To my left, was a wooden door with a keyhole that looked as though it would be a fit to the key. With my heart still pounding, I tried to open the door, but found it was indeed locked. I quickly slid the key into the hole, and the lock clicked.

"Oh. My. Gosh!" I could barely contain my excitement. Opening the door slowly, I found that it led to a tunnel. "I can't believe this." I threw caution to the wind and followed the path of the tunnel. It was cold, and eerie; my heart still pounded. As I walked, I couldn't help but wonder where I would end up. The tunnel curved, and though I wasn't brilliant with directions, I felt I was heading towards Lake Michigan from underneath the fort. Finally, I came to a dead end and another rickety ladder leading up to yet another trap door. I carefully climbed the ladder, and pushed at the trapdoor. It didn't budge.

"Dang it!" I exclaimed. Had I really come this far for nothing? I pounded on it with my shoulder in frustration. It moved slightly as dirt fell in my face, and with another push of my shoulder, it opened. I smiled to myself, and climbed out the door. I immediately felt the wind from the Straits of Mackinac on my face again. While I had been underground, the sky had darkened

9

and the stars were out. I turned and saw that the exit from the tunnel was right in front of the cannon platform.

"Excellent. An escape tunnel!" I had heard and read about tunnels like this, mostly during my travels down South, but it didn't take me long to sense that something wasn't right. It was quiet. Way too quiet. No sound of cars rushing by overhead, and the sounds I could hear were all coming from…behind me, from the fort. I could smell wood smoke, and the Mackinac Bridge…I quickly turned back. Was. Not. There. My stomach plummeted. I rubbed my eyes and looked again. Still no bridge. What had just happened?

CHAPTER TWO

I couldn't think straight. What was going on? Where was the bridge? I groped into my pocket for my phone. I had to call someone. Tell someone. But as I looked at my phone, all I saw was the 'No Service' signal.

"Why no service? I always get service here." Panic was beginning to set in. Pure and utter panic. The darkness around me worried me even more.

"Mademoiselle, can we help you?" I looked up. In my panic, I hadn't noticed three men striding towards me carrying lanterns. They were dressed like French fur traders, and looked more authentic than any I had ever seen. Even more so than the hardcore reenactors I had met. As they got closer, their stench made me realize that they were too authentic. The man who had spoken was quite young, too young to even shave. He was thin, and the rest of his features were hidden by a French-looking tricorn hat. While the outfit was familiar enough, it was almost identical to what Jem had been wearing earlier that day, it was his thick French accent that truly threw me.

"I...ohh...I." I had no idea what to say, what to do, how to react.

"Are you lost? Who do you belong to?" A second man asked. This one was massive, big, barrel-chested, and broad-shouldered. His voice was gruff and he spoke with a French accent as well. I quickly dropped my cell phone into my pocket with my extra battery stick, a much practiced move. However, the act was usually to hide the phone from visitors, not three unfamiliar men.

The third fur trader seemed to recognize what I had done. He was of average height, with a medium build and brown hair, and a scruffy beard. He was quite handsome, actually, and appeared to be a year or so older than me. Something about the way he looked at me made me calm. It was as if he knew something wasn't right either.

"Can it be?" He asked, as if he had suddenly recognized me. "Ma chere, is it you?" He strode toward me, recognition of sorts apparent on his face. His reaction confused me even more. I had no idea who he was, though there was something familiar about him. He set his trade gun and lantern down, wrapped me in a huge hug, and then surprised me by whispering in my ear. "I know where you're from. Just play along. Please."

The knowledge that someone could explain what was going on calmed and reassured me. I felt that I could trust him. When he pulled back to look at me, our eyes met and held. He had warm, brown eyes. I nodded.

"What's your name?" He mouthed.

"Christine Belanger." I whispered back.

"Beckwith, what is the meaning of this?" The bigger man asked.

"Barreau, this is my fiancé!" Brown Eyes turned, still holding my arm. "Miss Christine Belanger."

Fiancé? My stomach dropped again. *I'm not old enough to be anybody's fiancé. What the heck was going on? What had I gotten myself into?*

"Well, then. We'll leave you two alone." The thin man grinned. "Shall we tell your uncle that she is here?"

"Yes, tell him we'll be there shortly." He begged me with his eyes to continue to play along. I glanced over again towards the non-existent Mackinac Bridge. I had to trust him. I didn't know what else to do.

The other men headed toward a neighborhood that stood next to the fort. I knew from history that it had been like that prior to the fort being moved to the Island during the American Revolution, though those buildings hadn't been rebuilt. When the other men were out of earshot, I pulled out of Brown Eyes' embrace.

"Okay what in the world is going on? Where is the bridge? Who were those other guys? Who are you? Why did you tell them

12

we're engaged? I don't even know you." I tried not to let my panic show. It wasn't working.

He gently grasped my arm. "Slow down. I'll explain everything. At least everything that I can tell you. There are some things that I don't even have the answer to." He took a deep breath. "This is going to sound absolutely, unbelievably crazy, but you've traveled back in time."

"WHAT!" I exclaimed. It was true, there had been times that I wished I lived in a different century, yet I never dreamed that it would really ever happen. I didn't even know that it COULD happen.

"Shhh." He put a dirt-stained finger to my lips. I knocked his hand away.

"Don't shush me," I said, though I did lower my voice. "You can't drop a bomb like that on me and not expect me to react with disbelief." I shook my head. "Back in time?" As unbelievable as it sounded, it actually made sense, in a strange way. It would explain why the bridge was gone, why the men were dressed as they were, why it was so dark. I just couldn't believe that time travel was actually possible. Who would believe that?

"So who are you?" I asked.

"My name is Henry Beckwith. Folks here call me Henri. I'm living as a French trader." I realized that he had dropped his French accent once the men were out of earshot, although he still had a slight one.

"Beckwith? Henry Beckwith? As in the Henry Beckwith who, three years ago, went with his brother to break into Michilimackinac and then disappeared. Everyone thinks you're dead. That Henry Beckwith?"

"Yes, that Henry Beckwith. I assume you got down here through the tunnel, but where did you find the key?"

"I work at Colonial Mich. A coworker found it in the priest's garden and gave it to me to hold on to. My curiosity got the best of me so I went looking for the matching lock. The first place I thought to look was the priest's cellar, it just made sense." I thought for a moment, so many questions. "How did you know about the key?"

"It's how my brother and I got here as well." He straightened, picked up his gun and lantern in one hand and gave me a gentle tug

13

toward the neighborhood with the other. "Come on. I'll introduce you to my family."

I was quite lucky that Henri had been the one to find me. I followed him along the palisade wall to the neighborhood. Camps were set up everywhere. The smells were overpowering: food cooking, spices, gunpowder, wood smoke, animal pelts and body odor all together. I wasn't sure how long I would be able to handle the stench.

"This cannot be happening," I muttered.

"As I said earlier, I will explain everything, I promise," Henri said. "Though to be honest, I'm not sure if everything can be explained. I don't understand it myself, but Jacques might be able to fill in some blanks for you."

"Who is Jacques?" I asked. The area in and around the fort was more crowded than I had ever seen it.

"Jacques Evans. Around here, he's known as my uncle, but you may know him as Jack Evans."

I hesitated. "You don't mean Old Man Evans..." I lost my balance as a dirty, smelly trapper bumped into me. Henri's empty arm quickly steadied me. My breath caught again as I looked into his brown eyes, so warm they reminded me of hot chocolate. I quickly righted myself and Henri reached over and gave the man who had run into me a shove.

"Watch yourself!" He then took my arm again and we continued our walk.

"I apologize for him. All of them, really."

I shook my head. "No worries. I was just surprised is all."

"So you're used to getting knocked around?" He asked.

"I've played power forward for the Mackinaw City Comets varsity basketball team for the past two years. I can handle myself." *Though I sometimes wonder if certain people are right and the only reason I play is because my sister is the coach.* I shrugged the thought away. "So tell me, Jack Evans. Old Man Evans. Surely you know the legends of him back home."

"There are legends of him in this time period as well." Henri gave me a small smile and I decided that I liked it, but I got the feeling that he didn't do so very often. "You will meet him soon enough."

Henri kept his head down as he passed the British soldiers who were walking around on patrol. As we passed one trio of soldiers,

14

Henri tried to avoid them completely. One Redcoat stepped in front of us and blocked our path. He had broad shoulders, and stood a foot taller than Henri. Straight brown hair poked from under his black, army-issue tricorn hat. His gray eyes were cold and cocky. Henri slid one hand down to grasp mine, handed me the lantern in my other hand, and then held tight onto his trade musket. He gave my hand a slight squeeze.

"Well, Beckwith, what do we have here?" The Redcoat looked me up and down in a way that gave me the creeps.

"Sergeant Hugo, this is Miss Christine Belanger, my intended. I would thank you to let us pass and stay away from her in the future." Disdain dripped form Henri's voice.

"If she's French like you, I wouldn't want to pursue her socially anyways. However, this is a small community, Beckwith, and I highly doubt I can stay completely away from her." The soldier looked at Henri with absolute revulsion, as if Henri wasn't good enough to be breathing the same air as him. I quickly glanced at Henri, who was looking back at the soldier with complete hatred. His jaw clenched and he turned.

"Come on. Let's get you to Jacques."

I glanced behind at the soldier, Hugo. He was still watching us. I took a deep breath. Things had just gotten even more complicated.

I continued to follow Henri through the neighborhood back towards one of the dwellings. I took a deep breath. In real time, this area was a restroom, which suddenly made me think. Though I always said that I would and could live in a different time period, I knew the bathroom situation would give me pause. I didn't really want to use an outhouse or chamber pot. We walked through the open door. I looked around the small, dimly-lit room. One bed was tucked in the corner, and five people crowded around a small drop-leaf table.

"Good evening, everyone," Henri said. "I would like you all to meet Christine Belanger." He squeezed my hand. "My fiancé from back home." He gave a meaningful look to a grizzled old man with gray hair and tired-looking eyes. I assumed the man was Jacques, or 'Old Man Evans. Sitting to his left was a pretty native woman, who appeared to be his wife. Next to her was a beautiful, dark-complexioned young woman, a friendly-looking native boy a year or two younger than me, and another native boy who looked to be around the age of five or six.

The older woman stood and gracefully approached me. "Welcome, my dear." She took me in her arms and brushed each of my cheeks with a kiss. "I must admit, Henri alluded to a young woman from back home that he was fond of, but we had no idea it had progressed so far." She had a soothing, gentle voice and, though I had just met her, I felt immediately comfortable with her. I hated the thought of deceiving her, but knew I had to trust Henri. My secret was not just mine.

"Yes, thank you…" I didn't know what to say next. Luckily, Henri spoke up.

"I didn't want to say anything until she was actually here," he explained. "Just in case she never actually arrived."

"Of course." The older woman smiled again at me. "Please, excuse our not welcoming you properly. We would have been down at the lake to greet you and had a wonderful meal waiting for you had we known you were coming."

"Don't worry about it at all," I replied, touched by her caring.

"I am Aimée, Jacques's wife. My first husband, Pierre died years ago."

"He was killed, you mean," Henri said, a touch of anger in his voice.

"Henri, please." She shook her head, then focused her brown eyes on me. "Please meet the others in our family." She gestured to the beautiful young woman. "This is my daughter, Simone." The young woman smiled. Aimée continued introductions. "My son, Antoine." The teenager gave me a charming smile. He was extremely handsome, and was likely quite popular in the settlement. "And my grandson, Rémy." The boy came to stand next to Aimée and she put an arm around him.

"My papa's not here right now," the boy said, a somber look on his face. "He's stuck in the guardhouse."

"What?" Henri growled.

"Henri, please." Aimée warned. I immediately felt uncomfortable. Why was Aimée's son in the guardhouse and why was Henri so angry about it?

"What has he done now? Supposedly?" He turned to Jacques. "Why didn't you tell me?"

"Nothing you could have done to stop it," Jacques replied with a gruff voice. "Didn't want you going out there and losing your temper again."

Henri clenched his jaw. "What. Did. Cort. Do?"

"Same as always, Henri." Antoine stood. "He was being disrespectful to the British, giving that soldier, Hugo a hard time."

"And that is enough to keep him in the guardhouse?" I exclaimed. I couldn't believe it. I had learned that there was tension between the French and the British during this time period and in this place, but what Antoine was describing seemed unreasonable.

"Henri has been arrested for lesser offenses." Simone spoke softly. "Cort as well, and…" Tears welled in her eyes.

"Miss Belanger, you briefly witnessed the way the British acted towards us, but unfortunately, it is not contained to rudeness and suggestive commentary." Henri looked at me. "I am sorry you've been brought into the middle of all this."

"There must be a reason for it," Aimée said, wisdom in her voice. Jacques came and stood next to her, putting an arm around her.

"I agree with that," he said. "There is always a reason for what happens in our lives."

Henri blew out a breath.

Jacques continued, "Henri, there was a reason for you coming here, as I told you before, and there is a reason Miss Belanger is here now." He gave Henri a meaningful look. Henri shook his head.

"I need to go and see Cort. Try and get him out." Henri took a few steps towards the door, but Jacques stepped in front of him and placed a hand on his chest.

"You know that will do no good," Jacques insisted.

"I can't just sit here while he's trapped in the black hole!" Henri gave a half-hearted shove to Jacques's shoulders.

"Henri, think. What can you even do?" Aimée placed a hand on Henri's arm. "You know there is nothing we can do but wait."

Henri rested his hands on his hips, not meeting anyone's eyes. "I hate the waiting," he finally said, meeting Jacques's eyes. The old man gave a quick nod in my direction, never breaking eye contact with Henri. Henri clenched his jaw and turned to me.

"Miss Belanger, I know it's late, but would you like to take a stroll?" He asked.

I looked around at the family. I had so many questions for Henri, and I knew as some questions were answered more would come. A part of me wanted to go for a walk to get the answers, yet there was another part that wanted to simply go to bed and get some sleep. Perhaps then I would wake up and discover that all of this was some crazy dream. But that thought led me to realize…

"I just realized that there are some issues that I hadn't considered in all of this excitement. One being, where will I sleep while I am visiting?" How could Henri and I explain all of the holes that were bound to come up in my story once people started asking questions?

"You'll sleep on my pallet. We'll move it to Simone's side of the room up in the storage area." Henri seemed to have an answer for everything.

"I can't take your pallet," I protested.

"Of course you can," he replied. "And it's useless for you to argue with me." He nodded toward the narrow stairwell. "I realize it's not the finest of accommodations, but I wouldn't have you stay anywhere else."

I glanced toward Simone, who had a kind smile on her face.

"I assure you it will be no imposition," she said softly. "It will also be quite proper, though we will technically be in the same room. We pile all of the supplies up in the middle, so it is just as good as a wall."

"Well, all right." I smiled back at the young woman. She seemed so kind, yet there was a sadness about her. She couldn't be that much older than me, yet she seemed so much more mature than I was.

"Do you have any bags that need to be brought up?" Antoine asked with a charming smile. "I would be happy to help."

"No, she doesn't. The canoe her baggage was in capsized. Luckily, she was riding in a different one." With all of the voyageurs coming in, that would be a very plausible explanation. Henri had apparently thought of that as well.

"Yes, that's exactly it." I nodded, hoping I could remember all of these stories and keep them straight. I had never been that good of a liar.

18

"Very well," Antoine replied. "You let me know if I can do anything for you, Miss Belanger."

"Miss Belanger, about that stroll…" Henri looked at me and offered his arm. I took it and we stepped outside.

CHAPTER THREE

I was once again blown away by how boisterous and busy the fort was. The sounds and smells were still overpowering

"I cannot believe any of this," I said as we made our way around the rowhouse. "I'm not sure I will ever be able to believe this."

"I feel the same way," Henri admitted. "After three years, I figured I would be stuck here forever. I have accepted the fact that I will never make it back to the twenty-first century." He sighed. "Honestly though, I think about home all the time, yet I am so busy here just trying to survive, I don't have time to dwell on it." He shook his head. It was difficult to hear him with all of the noise surrounding them. Men talking loudly and laughing, many of them drinking. Another fur trader bumped into me, shoving me into Henri this time. His arms came around me and he pulled me behind him, facing the fur trader and pushing him away. The man slurred something in French and stumbled off.

"This wasn't the best of ideas," Henri grumbled. "Too many men drinking."

"What about Ste. Anne's?" I asked. "Would that be quiet enough for a conversation?"

"Yes, it probably would be." He pulled me in the direction of the church building. "Père Gibault isn't expected to arrive until tomorrow or the day after, so it should be empty now. It will be a fine place for a discussion." He led me into the church and we sat down on the benches that served as pews, facing each other. I smiled and looked around the beautiful church. It was always a favorite place of mine in the fort. The interior was big and open, and the altar and tabernacle up front were beautifully carved and painted in detail. It was always such a contrast to the primitive decorations that graced the rest of the fort.

Henri must have noticed my gaze. "It is beautiful in here. I must admit, I never thought I would miss attending weekly services as much as I have. I long to go to church with my family over at St. Anne's on the island. Such a beautiful building. It's strange to me that it won't even be built for another hundred years or so." He shook his head and looked around the church. "We all wait with anticipation for the traveling priest to come through." The lantern light cast flickering shadows onto the walls. "I would like to ask what has happened in the world since I've been here, but I'm not sure where we would even begin."

"That is true." I said. "I can tell you that most everyone thinks you and your brother are dead. That you were sneaking to the mainland when your canoe capsized. It was found on the Lake Michigan side of the straits, near McGulpin Point Lighthouse.

"So my mother and father think both their sons are dead." He clasped his hands in front of him and leaned his elbows on his knees. "Well, they are half-right."

His tone and words confirmed for me what I had been thinking and fearing. "Your brother did die."

"Yes." Henri stood and strode to the chest-high window that faced the north, toward the island. "And it was all my fault." He shook his head. "We had a plan, Mark and I. We wanted to sneak into the fort and hang an American flag, as a joke, in the British fort, you know. Mark was always really competitive with Abel Taylor, a kid from Mac City. It was my idea, a way to prank Abel. We made it to the mainland and snuck into the fort without any problems. It was after we had hung the flag that we found the old key. I was running back to the canoe and I tripped and fell in a garden behind the Commandant's House. The key turned right up and as most any boy would be, we were intrigued to know what it might open."

I pulled the very same key out of my pocket. I could easily understand why it could inspire curiosity.

"We found the passageway in the priest's cellar, as you described, almost as if drawn to it. We found ourselves in 1772. Only by the grace of God did we run into Jack Evans before anyone else. It would have been hard to explain our shorts and t-shirts to British soldiers or French traders." He shook his head. "I think Jim was just as surprised to see us as we were to see him. He took us in and told everyone we were his nephews from Montreal. It worked. People here never questioned it."

"So since I am from that same home, I am from Montreal as well." I stored that information in my mind.

"Yes, that is something you should know." Henri nodded, then turned to face me. He leaned against the wall and folded his arms over his chest. "We lived here fairly peacefully for a while. Mark and I both always loved the outdoors and camping, so we were able to adjust fairly easily. Jacques taught both of us his trade."

"Which is what, by the way?"

"He is a trader. He literally taught us trade."

I laughed and Henri smiled. I realized again that he didn't smile that often.

"What happened to Mark?" I asked.

"As you might have noticed, there are deep tensions between the British soldiers and the French traders."

"It's not hard to miss." As I thought about these tensions, I recalled the previous comment from Simone that Henri had been arrested before.

"I will admit, some of the soldiers are a decent sort, but the majority of them treat the civilians with contempt. They think nothing of physically abusing someone whenever they get the slightest whim and the smallest infraction can get you a beating or time in the black hole."

I shuddered at that thought. The black hole was creepy enough in the abstract when I described it to visitors at the fort. It was a hole dug underground, where the British kept prisoners accused of crimes. Just thinking about it made my heart pound. The dirt walls, feeling as though they were closing in on you. The damp, earthy smell all around you. I surely would have gone mad in minutes if I ever found myself in there. It was a cruel form of solitary confinement. "Has that happened to you?" I asked.

"Both, yes." His voice was quiet and he looked at his boots. "I would do anything to get Cort out of there. The black hole is…well, I must admit that I would prefer a beating over the mental torture of that dark, damp hole." He shook his head. "Like I said, the first year passed by relatively peaceful, but then a

23

Leftenant Callum Lewis arrived here." He glanced at me, brown eyes full of sorrow. "I hope you never run into that man, though it will be hard to avoid him. He is pure evil, Christine. And what's worse, he has developed an unhealthy obsession with Simone. He's never laid a hand on her, but he's just...creepy when they interact. She's terrified of being in his presence."

"Goodness." I wasn't sure what else to say.

"Yes. The problem was, Mark and Simone always had a special relationship. If I were to guess, I would say they were in love. Mark thought that if he and Simone were engaged, Lewis would back off. The two were to be married when the priest came around and all the preparations were ready."

"Of course." I nodded. "Did Mark's plan work?" Henri scoffed.

"They weren't engaged a fortnight before Lewis sicced his henchmen on Mark. Remington Hugo, he's the soldier that was leering at you earlier, he and some other soldiers created some trumped up charges to arrest Mark. When Mark resisted, Lewis had Hugo and the others beat him to a pulp." Henri clenched his jaw. "They made me watch, Christine, just because they knew how much it would hurt me and because they could. So I know from painful experience just how sinister these men can be." He ran a hand through his hair. "If we had been in our world, this never would have happened, and if it did, he would have gotten the medical help he needed, but now he's dead."

"I am so sorry, Henri." A part of me wanted to stand and go comfort him. "But you don't know for sure that he would have lived."

"I do, and since I'm the one who had the bright idea to...well...I know I am stuck here in 1775, but I won't rest until I make Lewis pay."

"Why...why does Lewis act this way, why does he do such malicious acts?"

"I don't know." Henri paced to the next window. "I do know that the man hates the French who live here. He's just plain deranged. He wants to eliminate all the French, and any metis with French blood."

"But Henri, why does he want the French gone?"

"I'm not sure." He sighed. "I am afraid you came at a time when your life could very well be in danger, Christine. I have felt

24

for a while that this situation would be coming to a head. If you ask Aimée or Jacques, they'd tell you that everything happens for a reason, so you must be here to help us."

"I can believe that." I shrugged, but really, I couldn't remember a time when my help seemed needed. Sure, Sadie insisted that she needed me as a friend, but I knew well that if I wasn't around, she would have no problem finding a new best friend. I knew my family loved me, but I have so many siblings that I was never really needed much. It was also obvious that the boys in my class didn't need me around, based on what I had overheard. *Pretty enough, but not worth the bother of dating.* That led me to remember something else that had been bothering me since I had gone back in time.

"Henri, why fiancé? What was the meaning of that?"

He sighed again. "It was the first thing I could think of. I'm sorry if that made you uncomfortable, but I just...I believe that will be the best way to keep you protected."

"And sister wouldn't have worked?" I asked.

He blushed. "Well, you were my first crush, so...I don't know, sister never crossed my mind."

I was taken aback. "Crush? I know you seem familiar to me, but where...where have we met before? And if you knew who I was, why did you ask my name when you found me?"

"I asked your name because, while I was fairly sure who you were, I wanted to be positive. As for us meeting before, until I was 12 or 13, my dad would come to the mainland to play slow pitch softball. He played against your dad a lot, and you would always be at the games, playing pickup basketball, football, or wiffleball. You were always able to keep up with the boys. I liked how you never backed down from them. I would join in when I was there and I thought you were always so good. I admired that. I always wanted to talk to you and hang out with you. To be honest, had I remained in the twenty-first century, I might have really tried to get your attention, as a friend first, of course." He blushed again and I felt my face redden as well.

"Well, I am incredibly thankful that you found me at the shore first and you realized what had happened to me." I shuddered thinking of what could have happened, the mistakes I could have made. "I imagine...I probably would have been arrested as a witch or something."

"Luckily, we're not in Massachusetts, but, as I'm sure you know, there are many French tales of ghosts and specters."

"Yes. *Lupe garus* and *feu follets*." I laughed, thinking of the French stories I had learned about in preparation for Fort Fright, an annual event where Colonial Michilimackinac was turned into a haunted fort. *Lupe garus* were werewolves and *feu follets* were will-o'-the-wisps.

"Yes. In fact, Jacques has made quite a name for himself in the French community as a *raconteur*."

"I don't believe I've heard that term before," I admitted.

"It's a special tale-teller among the French community." Henri explained. I nodded, then looked out one of the windows of the church.

"It is so different here. I mean, the layout is the same, yet..." I shook my head. "Everything is different. How have you been able to survive? You know, live for the past three years in a time that is so different from ours?"

"Luckily, Mark and I had Jacques to help. We were both always good students, and history interested us, so we had some knowledge of what to say and do. I tell you what, though, it has not always been easy." He pulled out a pocket watch. "I suppose I should get you back to Jacques house. I imagine you want to get some sleep." He offered his arm to me and I threaded my own through his.

It didn't take us long before we were back at Jacques's rowhouse, but when we arrived, everyone else in the family was already asleep. The fire was down to smoldering embers and all the candles were blown out. As Henri led me up the stairs, I pulled back on his arm.

"I have nothing for pajamas," I said. The situation I was in was continually throwing me curveballs. I had traveled back in time, and found two other men who had done the same, men who people back home believed were dead. But at least I wasn't completely alone, and I had a basic enough understanding of colonial life. I could get by until I figured out how to get back to the twenty-first century. I had to get by.

"I have an idea." Henri continued up the stairs into the storeroom. He tried to keep the lantern covered enough not to disturb the sleeping Simone, Antoine and Rémy. The light threw ghoulish shadows on the walls, made even more eerie with all of the trade goods and bundles piled everywhere. Someone must have already dragged Henri's pallet to Simone's side, as there was an empty pallet and blanket there.

"I am sure I can get you something proper tomorrow," Henri said quietly. "But if you are really in need of something for tonight..." He went to a wooden trunk and pulled out a t-shirt. The front said Mackinac Island Lakers Football. He handed it to me.

"The Lakers have never had a football team," I said, looking at Henry, who gestured for me to turn the shirt and look at the back, which read: 'Undefeated since 1962'.

"Exactly. You can't beat a team that doesn't exist." Henry smiled one of his rare smiles. "Mark loved that t-shirt. He was wearing it when we came over. Or went back, I suppose." He shook his head. "It might be a bit big on you, but that should work for sleeping. I'm sorry I don't have any bottoms for you."

"No worries there." I hiked up my skirt to show him my Mackinaw City Comets basketball shorts.

"Well, that's not very historically accurate."

"Don't tell my boss, but I always have these on under my skirts. I love being historical, but I also like comfort."

"There's nothing wrong with that, and it works in your favor for sure this time," he replied.

"I suppose so." I smiled.

"I'll let you get some sleep. You have a good night, Christine."

"You too, Henri. And thank you for all of your help."

CHAPTER FOUR

I woke up to the call of a rooster. I groaned and rolled over to see Simone's pallet empty and little Remy sitting on a bale of fur, watching me.

"Mornin', Miss Christine," he said.

"Where is everyone else?" I asked, rubbing my eyes.

"Up and working already," he replied. "I think Uncle Henri went to get my Papa." He jumped off the bale. "I'll go and tell grand-mère you're awake."

I rolled off the pallet and began to pull on my skirt and shirtwaist. The heat up here was stifling. I was surprised I had been able to sleep at all. Traveling almost 250 years back in time must have tired me out. I went down the stairs and saw Aimée and Simone already preparing meals for the day.

"Good morning, Miss Belanger," Aimée said. "I hope you slept well."

"I did, thank you." I nodded. "Though I must say, I always thought all family members stayed in the main room and no one slept upstairs." The words were out of my mouth before I realized how strange they might sound. "I mean, that's what we heard happened on the frontier."

"Well, we do stay together during the colder months to conserve energy, but it can get to hot if we all stay in one room during the summer." Simone explained.

"I suppose that makes sense," I replied. "So, what can I do to help? Chop vegetables for soup? Gather firewood or water?

Mend clothes?" I clapped my hands together, eager to start working.

"You should probably break your fast first." Simone mixed batter for what appeared to be biscuits. She nodded towards the fireplace. "There's some sagamety on the fire."

Sagamety. Wonderful. I pasted on a fake smile. "That sounds delicious. I am rather hungry." Hungry enough to eat sagamety, or cornmeal mush, a breakfast that I had all too much growing up at home and even more earlier that summer, working at the fort.

Aimée grabbed a wooden bowl and spooned me up some breakfast. I desperately wished for cinnamon or brown sugar to sweeten the food.

"Thank you." I sat down and quickly ate. It may not have been tasty, but I knew it would fill me up until the midday meal. I brought the dish to the wash pail and quickly washed and dried it.

"You're not afraid of hard work. That is good," Aimée said.

Simone smiled. "Yes, when Henri told us he had a fiancé from Montreal, I wondered if you would be a spoiled little rich girl."

"Henri spoke of me before yesterday?" I asked, puzzled.

"Nothing specific, but every time a young woman from the community expressed interest in him, he told them he was already promised to a woman from back home." Aimée explained. "So you shouldn't worry, Miss Belanger. He has been true to you these past three years."

"I never thought otherwise," I said. Henri had given me the impression of being a really good guy. He could stand to lighten up a bit, but he had been extremely helpful and very trustworthy so far. "So what can I do to help?"

Aimée pushed some carrots and a knife towards me. "Go ahead and cut these up. We're having potato stew for the midday meal."

"Perhaps Jacques and Antoine will get lucky while hunting and we can add some meat later."

"I do love venison," I said. "My brothers enjoy hunting and my mother has some really nice recipes for it."

"How many brothers do you have?" Aimée asked.

"Two brothers, and three brothers-in-law who are as close as actual brothers." I replied.

"My goodness, you have quite the large family," Simone exclaimed.

"Yes, I am the youngest of six. All of my siblings are quite successful." I hesitated. "Married well, that is." I couldn't tell these two women that one of my sisters was a doctor, one an accountant for a big company in Gaylord, and one a beloved teacher and coach. Aimée and Simone would question that in this time period. "I already have six nephews and three nieces between them all."

"Mon Dieu, you must miss them terribly," Aimée said. My heart sank as it hit me that I may never see my family again. It was true, I sometimes felt as though they didn't need me around, but I would miss them desperately, and the news my sister Rachel had just shared with me the other day...would I ever get a chance to snuggle and hold that child?

"Yes, I do." I wiped a tear from my eye.

"How did they feel about you coming out here?" Simone asked.

"Oh, they were fine with it," I lied. "They'll miss me, to be sure, but I am not really needed so much."

"That cannot possibly be true, ma fille," Aimée said. "They need you, but I believe you are needed here in Michilimackinac even more. Especially with the troubles we are having. Henri always takes it upon himself to help correct the situation. You can be of great comfort to him."

"Yes, and hopefully the priest will come by soon so you two can be married." Simone gave me a small, knowing smile. "Then you could be even more of a comfort to him, oui?"

My face heated at her insinuation. How long would we have to act out this charade of being engaged? I wasn't ready to be married. Not at all, especially not to Henri. He may be one of the best-looking guys I had ever met, and I felt quite comfortable with him, but I had only known him for a day.

"Well, he and I, well...he has some work to do before we are able to be together first. That is what we were speaking of last night."

"Ahh, so he told you of the plot of land he plans to build a cabin on?" Aimée asked.

"Yes, of course," I lied again, hoping they didn't ask any more detailed questions that I couldn't answer. "I hope to see it soon."

"I'm sure he's anxious to show it to you. He has told us about it, but Jacques is the only one who knows where it is." Simone

31

finished mixing the dough. "Come with me to get some water. I can show you some of the fort too. You likely didn't see much of it last night."

"I did not," I said, wiping my hands on my apron. "I would love to walk with you."

"Splendid," Aimée said. "I will feel much more at ease with you both going." She gave Simone a meaningful look.

"Mère, I'll be just fine. It has been weeks since there's been an incident, at least with me."

"Well, the two of you be careful."

"Of course, Mère," Simone said as she walked out the door and picked up two buckets and a yoke to carry them. I grabbed a second yoke and buckets, knowing just how much easier the device made carrying water.

"Today is washing day, so we'll need these four buckets and then more." Simone explained as we walked. The neighborhood and camps were quiet this morning. Men who had been socializing late into the night were still sleeping. British soldiers stood on guard as we made our way through the path to Lake Michigan.

"I am glad it's warm out," I said. "I would hate to wade into the water when it's freezing outside."

"That does make doing laundry less desirable," Simone agreed. "I'll be so glad when Rémy can take this chore over.'

"That will be nice. He seems like a good kid…I mean…child." I hoped Simone didn't recognize my slip-up. How many times would I do that?

"Yes, he is," Simone agreed. "It's good that Cort stayed here in Michilimackinac. He almost left after he lost his wife."

"I see."

We made our way to the edge of the lake and set our buckets down. Simone bent to remove her moccasins as I overturned one of my wooden buckets to sit and remove my shoes and stockings. I looked forward to wading into the cool water of the straits.

We continued talking after we filled our buckets and walked back toward the house, this time going through the fort, as Simone told me she wanted to bring some water to an elderly gentleman in one of the row houses there. Simone was a wonderful person to talk with, and I believed she would become a good friend and confidante.

As we passed the guardhouse, I noticed Simone got a little quieter. I looked to see what the issue may be. I recognized the soldier named Remington Hugo. He leaned his musket against the guardhouse wall. My heart sped up as he sauntered over to us. Simone tried to speed up her pace to get past him, but the burly man stepped right in front of her and grabbed her arm.

"Woah, there, Miss Lefevre. I wanted to have some words with you." He jerked her towards him. I froze. What should I say, what could I do?"

"Hey, now…" My weak words were drowned out by Hugo.

"Why are you trying to avoid me, girl?" He spoke softly, but I could still hear him. Two more British soldiers approached, one from behind me, one to the other side of Simone. I felt caged, my heart pounded even louder in my chest.

"Sergeant, please let us pass." She moved to get around him, but he grabbed her shoulder with his other hand and shook her.

"Please!" Simone begged as her yoke fell from her shoulders. The water buckets crashed to the ground and water splashed at her feet. I took a step towards Simone, but the Redcoat behind me grabbed me and held me back. It was all I could do not to drop my own water.

"Picking on defenseless women again, Hugo?" An unfamiliar voice called out. I looked over to see a very confident young man with smooth black hair pulled back in a ponytail and a Native American complexion approach us.

"This is no concern of yours, boy." Hugo shook Simone again.

"You made it my concern when you decided to accost a member of the Lefevre family. Is it not enough that you already have her brother in the pit? You must harass her and her friend as well?" His eyes briefly met mine, kind, brown eyes.

"I'll give you one more chance to walk away, Lafontaine."

"Raphael, please…" I could tell Simone was trying to hold back tears, but I couldn't tell if she was begging him to stay or leave.

"Or you'll do what, Hugo?" The young man taunted the soldier. Hugo spun and threw his fist into the young man's stomach. Raphael doubled over and the other two British soldiers quickly moved to hold him up.

"Please, don't!" Simone called out. I wasn't sure what to say or do, but I couldn't just stand there. Sergeant Hugo continued beating the young man, hitting his face and stomach repeatedly as the two other soldiers held him up. Just as I decided to jump into the fight, Henri came barreling into the mix, tackling Hugo with a wrap-up and takedown that would make John Cena proud. The other soldiers abandoned the young man, who crumpled to the ground, and they both jumped on Henri, picking up with him where they left off on the other young man. Simone hastened to the young man to help him, and just as I was about to try and help Henri, a gunshot cracked the air. I spun around and saw two new Redcoats. One looked to be in charge, with aristocratic posture, a powdered wig and a walking cane. The other man held a smoking pistol, pointed in the air. I was relieved to realize that no one had been hit by the bullet.

"Desist now." The white-haired officer looked at the soldiers who had been beating the civilians. One of the Redcoats who had been holding Henri shoved him into the mud that had formed from the spilled buckets of water.

"Take care of this, Leftenant." The white-haired officer spoke to the soldier standing next to him, then strode back towards the commandant's house.

"Yes, sir, Major DePeyster." The other soldier spoke in a low, threatening voice as he holstered his pistol and strode toward the guardhouse. He stepped over the young man that Simone was trying to tend to and came to stand directly in front of Henri, who was already looking worse for the wear. Blood dripped from a cut on his forehead and a split lip, and his right eye was already starting to darken. I held my breath as the soldier stood there for what seemed like a full minute, then drew back his fist and punched him in the face, then kneed him between the legs. I couldn't help but cry out.

"Throw him in the black hole." The Leftenant who had come outside with Major DePeyster commanded.

"Leftenant Lewis, what about Lefevre? He's still in there." One of the Redcoats, a Sergeant, who had been holding Henri spoke up.

"That matters not to me. They can both spend time in there."

My stomach sank. It would be bad enough with just one person in that pit, but two? I would go mad with claustrophobia.

"No, please, Leftenant." Simone stood and approached the officer. "Please don't put them both in there." A tear fell from her eye. "If there's any decency in you, please don't put both of them in the hole."

The soldier looked down at Simone. I recalled how Henri had told me that Leftenant Lewis had an unhealthy obsession with Simone. Would he listen to her?

CHAPTER FIVE

"I suppose Lefevre has been in there long enough," Leftenant Lewis said. "Remove him and throw Beckwith in."

I briefly met Henri's pained eyes as the two soldiers dragged him into the guardhouse. As I took a step towards Simone, who was helping the young man sit up, Leftenant Lewis turned to me and froze me with his cold eyes.

"You must be Miss Christine Belanger, newly arrived from Montreal."

"Yes, sir, and how did you know that?" I asked.

"You will quickly learn that nothing happens in this fort or the surrounding areas that I don't know about. I would advise you to keep your fiancé under control." He spun around and marched away. The other soldiers resumed their posts.

"Is he all right, Simone?" I knelt next to her and the young man.

"If I wasn't in so much pain, I would feel as if I'd died and gone to Heaven, surrounded by such lovely angels." The young man gave me a charming smile through his battered face.

"Christine, please meet my cousin, Raphael Lafontaine." Simone and I helped the man stand. "He is a voyageur."

"I am pleased to meet you, Mr. Lafontaine," I replied.

"You must be Henri's little secret." Raphael clutched his side. "The man's my closest friend but he never once mentioned he was courting someone, much less asked a woman to come here to the wilderness to be his bride."

"Henri is a private person. It doesn't surprise me at all." I replied with a smile.

"Aye, that's true." He grimaced.

"Should we get you to a surgeon?" I asked, hoping the fort had one. I searched my brain to see if I could recall the exact information.

"Ahh, no, he won't be able to do anything. Just bring me to Tante Aimée. She'll do a much better job tending my wounds."

"You're right about that," Simone replied, then turned toward me. "I can help Raphael and get one of the buckets if you can manage to get the others and the yokes."

"Of course," I replied. "My buckets are still full, but I think I can manage that. I can gather more water so you can help your mère care for Mr. Lafontaine."

"Not by yourself, you won't," Raphael stated firmly. "If what you just experienced wasn't a good enough indication, then nothing is."

"Well, we need water." My eyes drifted towards the guardhouse door as I gathered the buckets and yokes and we began to walk toward the Evans home. "How long will they leave Henri in there?" I asked quietly.

"As long as Lewis wants," Raphael replied. "We are at his mercy, unfortunately." He hobbled alongside Simone.

"He doesn't seem to show much of that," I muttered.

"You are very astute, Miss Belanger," Raphael said. "Not even here a full day and you have a keen sense of what's going on around here."

"It doesn't take long," Simone added as we entered the Evans home. "Mère, we need some help."

Aimée immediately began to tend Raphael. Just as Simone helped him to one of the chairs, a wide-shouldered Native burst into the room. He had a firm jaw, stoic expression, and wore his long, shiny black hair in a messy braid. He also sported a black eye.

"Cort! They let you out." Aimée smiled in gratitude.

"Yes, but only because they needed room for Henri." Cort Lefevre spoke in a deep, gravelly voice.

"I'm guessing that's the reason Raphael is in this state." Aimée sighed.

38

"Just the opposite, Mère." Simone helped her mother clean Raphael's wounds. "Hugo and his men were harassing Christine and me, so Raphael stepped in to help. The soldiers started beating Raphael and Henri tried to stop them. Commandant DePeyster brought a stop to everything but Lewis threw Henri into the black hole."

"Mon deu, what will they do next?" Aimée shook her head and continued helping Raphael.

"Who are you?" Cort looked at me, distrust apparent in his face.

"This is Christine Belanger, she arrived last night from Montreal." Simone smiled supportively at me. "She is promised to Henri."

"A woman comes to visit Henri, a women we have never even heard him speak of, and no one questions this?" The man's face remained impassive and unable to read. It was unnerving.

"I don't think we can blame him for not mentioning that someone this lovely was a part of his life." Raphael chuckled. "He wanted to keep her to himself because he knew that once she met me, she would like me better, mon ami?"

"Yes, that must be it." I smiled, trying not to show him how much his flattery affected me. Guys as smooth and attractive as Raphael always made me discombobulated.

"Hmm." Cort shrugged and looked around the one-room house. "Where's Remy?"

"Out hunting with Jacques and your brother." Aimée answered.

"Thank you for caring for him." Cort nodded. "Jacques wanted me to go and check with Wilger and Lionel, so I'll go and do that right now."

Simone must have noticed the confused look on my face. "Wilger and Lionel are Jacques's business partners." She explained as Cort walked out the door. "Don't you worry about Cort, Miss Belanger." Raphael smiled. "He's always cross."

"He has reason to be." Simone spoke gently, then looked at me. "Cort is distrustful of all strangers. With losing his wife and our father, well…" She looked at her mother, who remained quiet. "Well, we all know his death wasn't an accident like the British army determined it to be."

"Simone, please. Let's not dredge up old memories." Aimée straightened as she finished dressing Raphael's wounds. "And you, young man, are free to go, but you must take it easy for a few days."

"Merci, Tante Aimée." Raphael stood. "I shall go and see if there is any way to get Henri out, or at the very least, discover when he will be released."

"May Christine and I go with you?" Simone asked. "While you're talking with the British, we can refill our water, then you can accompany us back."

"That would make me feel much more at ease," Aimée added.

"I will indeed be your protector, ladies." Raphael smiled. It seemed a bit nonsensical that he had just been beaten up, yet he was offering to be our bodyguard.

"I do hope you can manage to get Henri out soon." I followed Simone and Raphael. "That black hole sounds positively dreadful."

"It is." Raphael nodded.

"You've been down there?" I asked.

"Practically every Frenchman has been in that hole since Lewis has been here." Raphael informed me. "I've been able to avoid it so far, but only by the grace of God."

"Well, that is the only good thing I've heard about this situation." I replied.

"Unfortunately, Henri spends more time in there than most men." Simone said, looking toward the guardhouse. "He doesn't like to see injustices occur."

"I think that's an admirable quality," I replied.

"Not necessarily." Raphael stopped at the guardhouse. "You two go down to the lake and I will see what I can do about Henri."

Simone and I continued to the lake. Life in Mackinaw was much more dire than I ever imagined.

Later that evening, Raphael came back to the Evans home. He was able to see the commandant and had been told that Henri would be released the following day. I couldn't fathom how

Raphael had managed to get that promise, but was glad nevertheless.

"Miss Belanger, I am going to bring your fiancé some food. I believe, with your help, I can manage to do that."

I looked at the rest of the family. Everyone was settling in for the evening. Cort and Remy had gone to their home farther out in the suburbs. I was getting a little stir crazy. "You may go with Raphael," Jacques said. "I trust him."

I nodded. I had immediately felt at ease with him myself, but did wonder at his confidence in getting some food to Henri. The British wanted to punish him, and likely wouldn't be keen on allowing him food.

"All right, then." Raphael smiled, took my arm, and we slipped out into the fading light.

The fort was crowded, as it had been last night, but again, the traders were too busy socializing to really notice the two of us. Raphael slipped a napkin-wrapped packet into my hands when we neared the guardhouse. "I'll distract the soldiers that are on duty, you slip inside and drop Henri the package."

"All right." I nodded, my heart pounding. I had never been one for sneaking around, but if we could bring Henri some comfort, I had to take a chance. I peered around the side of the guardhouse.

I didn't recognize the two soldiers posted to the building. I thought back to all my training and knowledge of the fort and realized that I couldn't remember how many Redcoats were stationed here. And did people even use the term 'Redcoat' yet?" My automatic reaction was to pull out my phone and Google the information, but that wasn't going to happen.

I was so lost in my thoughts that I almost missed the fact that Raphael had the guard's complete attention. I wasn't sure how he had done that, but I had to act now, before I lost my chance-or my nerve.

I slipped into the guardhouse. My eyes had adjusted enough to the darkness that the glow from the embers in the fireplace was enough for me to find my way around. I quickly made my way to the back corner where I knew the black hole was.

"Henri!" I whispered. I couldn't see anything in the pitch black pit.

41

"Christine, what are you doing here?" Henri sounded weak and a little angry.

"We brought you food. Raphael is distracting the soldiers."

"Of course he is."

"Here comes the food." I dropped the bundle down between the bars and heard it hit the ground with a thud. "How are you doing?"

"Miss Belanger?" Raphael darted into the room. "We got lucky. A brawl broke out and the guards went to break it up. We've got to go!" He grabbed my arm. "Thanks for helping today, mate!" He called down to Henri. "I'll see you out tomorrow."

"Raphael!" Henri called out, but Raphael ignored him and pulled me out of the guardhouse.

"All right, now let's get you back to the Evans's." Raphael loosened his grip, then suddenly tightened and pulled me into the alleyway between the church and blacksmith shop.

"Raphael, what…" My voice was cut off as Raphael covered my mouth with his hand.

"Shhhh." He whispered into my ear as he tried to shield me from something. It was then that I heard the talking.

"Mr. Green will be here in ten days' time, and DePeyster leaves tomorrow. He'll be gone a fortnight, and I will be in charge. That's when we act." I couldn't see who was speaking, but I recognized the low British voice of Callum Lewis.

"How'd you get DePeyster to leave the fort for that long?" If I had to guess, I would say that voice belonged to Remington Hugo.

"I have my ways. I have been laying plenty of groundwork and the commandant, the fool, trusts me." Lewis chuckled. "Sometimes you have to play a long game, Hugo."

"And your plan is still to destroy all of the French living here?"

I gasped at the words. Luckily, Raphael's hand was still on my mouth, muffling the sound.

"That's always been my plan. The French and their half-breed children should have never been allowed to stay here after we procured this land, and won the fort back in 1761. Those frogs have no right to be here and it is my mission to eradicate them from the area."

"And DePeyster? How will you justify killing him?"

"A casualty of war," Lewis answered. "There is always bound to be a noble death for a worthy cause."

"And having Olly kill him with his favored weapon will lay blame at the foot of the Indians," Hugo chuckled. "Brilliant idea, Leftenant.

Who was Olly? I wondered. I hadn't heard that name before.

"Indeed," Lewis replied. "Now, you know what you must do. Be off."

Both soldiers marched away, in different directions from the sound of it. Raphael slowly took his hand from my mouth and backed away. I couldn't believe what I had just heard.

"Did you hear…?"

Raphael took a deep breath. "I believe Henri has been right this whole time. Lewis wants to destroy all of the French here."

I gripped Raphael's forearm. "We must tell someone. Could we go to the commandant right now?" He shook his head.

"Even if we could get an audience with him, DePeyster would never believe us. I'm just a voyageur and son of a French trapper and you are a newcomer who is engaged to a trader. Even as respected as Jacques is, he wouldn't be taken seriously. Besides, you heard Lewis. DePeyster already trusts him too much." He took my arm in his and we began walking towards the land gate.

"We can talk with Jacques and see what he thinks, and Henri tomorrow."

"What about your own parents?" I asked. I had been wondering about his family since I had met him.

"Maman died years ago. Sickness. Papa, he is likely having too much of a celebration with his trade partners to care. When all the trappers, traders and voyageurs get together, I seldom see him." He shrugged as if it was no big deal, but I could sense that it bothered him.

"I'm sorry." I didn't know what else to say.

"It is not a unique situation," he said, "and I am used to it. The whole fort community has been watching over me for as long as I can remember, especially my Tante Aimée." He smiled as if reminiscing. "In spite of all the turmoil you have witnessed in the short time you have been with us, Miss Belanger, there are many good people here. Please do not judge us by some of the British and their actions. We have no control over their behavior."

"Of course not," I replied, "I completely understand."

43

"Good." He stopped in front of the Evans door and waited for me to enter the house. When I entered the room, Jacques and Aimée were still awake, sitting in front of the fire.

"How is Henri?" Jacques asked. "Were you able to speak with him?"

"Not much," I admitted, "but we got him the food, and Mr. Evans, we heard the most terrible plot being discussed."

Raphael and I told Jacques and Aimée what we had overheard. The two adults listened, not showing any emotion.

"The problem is, we can't just tell DePeyster. Even if we could get an audience with him, he'd never believe us," Raphael said.

"Not coming from any of the French, he wouldn't." Jacques agreed. "The tensions have been rising for some time. I'm not surprised it's finally coming to a head like this."

"But what can we do?" I asked. Raphael gave me a curious look and I realized he likely wasn't used to a girl speaking up in this way. Jacques smiled.

"I'll talk with you both and Henri tomorrow. Raphael, make sure you come by early," Jacques said.

"I'll hang around the guardhouse tomorrow until they release Henri."

"Very good." Jacques nodded and Raphael turned and kissed my hand.

"It was a pleasure spending time with you tonight, Mademoiselle Belanger." He gave me a charming smile.

"You as well, Monsieur Lafontaine." I smiled back. "I look forward to seeing you tomorrow."

"But of course," he replied, then walked out the door.

I sighed and immediately felt tired. I didn't even know what time it was. I felt so lost without my phone.

"You've had a long day, Christine. Why don't you go on up to bed?" Aimée suggested. "Simone went up just before you and Raphael returned, so she probably hasn't turned down the lantern yet."

"All right. Thank you." I trudged up the stairs. Aimée was right. Simone had braided her hair for the evening and was paging through what looked like a journal.

"I thought I heard you come in." She closed the book and smiled in her gentle, comforting way. "How is Henri?"

44

"I didn't see him, of course, but he sounded well enough." I took off my bonnet, pulled my hair out of its ties, then finger-combed it. "I cannot wait to get out of these stays." I groaned. I usually took the corset-like article of clothing off as soon as I could. This had been the longest I had ever worn them and the boning, or in my case, the extra-large zip ties, were digging into my skin.

"Raphael is quite the charmer, is he not?" Simone said. I took my clothes off, down to my chemise.

"I suppose he is." I replied after a brief hesitation. "But remember, I am engaged to Henri, you know. Raphael cannot charm me from my intended."

"Your fiancé, yes." Simone sounded as if she didn't quite believe me. "Come, let me brush your hair."

I sat on her pallet and turned my back to her.

"You need not pretend with me, Mademoiselle Belanger. I am fairly certain I know where you truly come from, and if that is the case, I'd gather Henri told everyone you were his fiancé to protect you."

"I don't know…" I had no idea how to reply.

"I realize you are likely on guard, based on all you have experienced since being here. However, you can trust me. I was engaged to be married to Henri's brother, you know. Mark told me everything, though I am not sure I understand it all. It is quite confusing."

"I know I don't understand it all," I muttered as Simone brushed my hair. "I just know how lucky I am that Henri was the first person to see me. It could have been much more difficult." I sighed. "Who else knows?"

"Mark only told me," she replied. "Jacques, of course knows, and I believe my mother knows your story about being from Montreal is false, but I'm not sure if she knows everything. Perhaps Jacques told her as Mark told me."

"Perhaps," I replied as she finished her work. "Thank you for doing this." It had been years since my mother had brushed my hair for me and it was so relaxing.

"Of course." She smiled gently. "I suppose we should both be getting to sleep."

"Yes, I think that's a good idea." I curled up on Henri's pallet and quickly fell asleep, with no idea just how long of a day tomorrow would be.

CHAPTER SIX

The next day began like the previous one, though I did wake up earlier. I choked down some sagamety for breakfast and helped Aimée and Simone prepare the midday meal.

"You seem quite at home in the kitchen, Christine," Aimée commented.

"Oh, I love cooking!" I exclaimed. "I wish I were able to cook more." The moment I spoke the words, I realized they would sound strange to colonial women who worked hard to cook every day. Even though Simone knew the truth and Aimée likely suspected something, I had to be more careful. "It's just that I'm always asked to do so many other things." I added.

"I understand," Aimée said with a smile.

"If you have the correct supplies, I would love to make you one of my favorite recipes." I grinned at the thought. "Cinnamon apple bread.'

"That sounds delicious." Simone said. "We'll try and get you what you need."

I leaned over the fire, pulled out the crane that extended over the flames and stirred the bouillabaisse, also known as fish soup. It smelled wonderful, with bacon, onions and carrots. Cooking truly was something I wished I could do more of. Even at home, my favorite place to be was in the kitchen. My family always gathered around the peninsula counter and nearby kitchen table, talking and laughing and teasing each other. I gulped back some tears. Would I ever see my family again? What do they think happened to me? I wished there was some way or somehow to let them know I was all right.

"Food smells good."

We all looked up to see a bruised and battered Henri enter the house.

"They let you out already?" I asked, glad to see him.

"They did." He nodded. "Not quite sure what Raphael said or did, but I'm free."

"Until the next time you irritate a British soldier," Simone scolded.

"Yes, that's true." Henri sat down and Aimée brought him a bowl of sagamety. "Thank you, Aunt Aimée."

"Of course." She brushed back a lock of his hair as if he was a little boy. "I'll get some comfrey for those cuts." He nodded and she walked out back to the garden.

"I thought Raphael would be with you." I said, mixing some dough for biscuits, or baps as they were called here. "He said he wanted to come over here to talk with you and Jacques. We heard some distressing news last night after bringing you food." I filled him in on the conversation we heard between Lewis and Hugo.

"Raphael should never have brought you to the guard house," he grumbled. "I just knew Lewis had something dastardly planned. If only we could somehow get DePeyster to believe us." He clenched his jaw.

"I've been thinking about that," I told him quietly as I sat next to him. "I could use the fact that I'm new around here and try to get close to one of the British soldiers, try and find out more details about their plan, or who else is a part of it."

Henri shook his head. "Absolutely not."

I was about to retort when Aimée returned to the room.

"Henri, you didn't forget about the wedding today, did you?" She asked, then turned to me. "You will join us, of course, Christine."

"I'd love to," I replied. I had watched and even participated in colonial wedding reenactments while working at the fort. It was always one of the best events.

"Good. We'll head over right after we clean up here. The soup will hold until later." Aimée smiled.

Not much later, I sat in Ste. Anne's Church, smiling with the rest of the congregation.

"The bride is Marie Anne Cardin and the groom is François Maurice de la Fantaisie." Henri whispered to me. He had washed up for the occasion, but still had cuts and bruises all over his face.

"You have to be joking." I smiled. The wedding I was about to witness in real life was the same wedding reenacted by the fort at Colonial Michilimackinac. I was overwhelmed with giddiness.

"No, I'm not," Henri replied. "Are those names significant to you?"

"Oh, just a little," I would explain in more detail later, but at that moment, I wanted to fully experience the event. As I had always imagined, the bride Marie Anne, was pretty in her long, light blue dress with a full skirt. Her groom, François, was quite handsome in his maroon, knee-length coat, brown waistcoat and white shirt. Père Gibault stood in front and gave advice to the bride and groom.

"Jesus Christ gave his life for the Church." The priest proclaimed. "The Church is the Bride of Christ, and Christ's self-sacrificing love for the Church is an example for all married couples to follow."

Henri shifted nervously next to me. I understood his uneasiness. As far as anyone else here was concerned, Henri and I were engaged, and would soon be saying the same vows. The thought made me very aware of his actions.

After the vows had been spoken, we moved to the parade grounds, where food and drink were available for the guests of the newlyweds.

"So it won't be long before you and Henri are in this position." Simone smiled in a teasing manner.

"Yes, I suppose so." I smiled back. "At least as far as everyone else is concerned." I looked around, making sure we wouldn't be overheard. "I do appreciate you keeping my secret."

"It is no problem at all," Simone replied.

The two musicians began tuning up their instruments, a fife and a fiddle.

"Ahh, the fun is about to begin," Simone said. "Do you know any of our dances, Miss Belanger?"

"I think I know enough to get by," I replied. "And I'm a quick learner."

"Well, we're lining up for the paddle dance. It's easy enough." Simone took my hand. I was relieved. This was one dance that I did know. Marie Anne stood at the head of the line, flanked by her groom on one side and her stepbrother, Monsieur Ainsse on the other. The women lined up on one side and the men faced us, leaving an aisle for the dancers. One of the men handed Marie Anne a paddle from a canoe. The musicians began playing *En Roulant*. The dancers began clapping along, and the dance began. Marie Anne glanced at her stepbrother, then handed him the paddle, took her husband's hands and the two sashayed sideways down the aisle. Monsieur Ainsse took a step over and the first two women in our line stood next to him. He then had the option of which lady he wanted to dance with. Whoever had the paddle held the power.

When it was my turn, I stood next to a man that I had just met, Mr. DuBois. He handed me the paddle and danced with the other woman, who I understood to be his wife. The next two men in line were Raphael and Henri. I looked back and forth at them, and was about to hand the paddle to Raphael when he reached for my hands. Henri was forced to take the paddle as Raphael and I sashayed down the aisle. When we reached the end, Raphael spun me around and we each returned to our lines. I looked to Henri just in time to see him skip down the aisle with a young girl, no older than ten, leaving Simone holding the paddle. The girl looked ecstatic that Henri had chosen her, and I was touched by his gesture. The dance continued for a while, and when it was finished, Henri took my arm and steered me toward the refreshment table.

"Are you thirsty, after all that dancing?" He asked.

"Yes, but I'm not sure wine is a good idea," I replied. "The only time I've ever had alcohol is the wine in church."

"Christine, I..." Henri glanced at Raphael, who was flirting with a pretty girl a year or so younger than me. "Be careful with Raphael. I love him like a brother, but something's been off about him since he's come back to the fort this summer."

The comment threw me off just a bit. I hadn't detected anything wrong. However, I thought of Dylan Rodriguez and his buddies, and was reminded that I didn't have the best judgment when it came to guys.

"What do you think caused the change?" I asked.

"It could be any number of things," Henri admitted. "But I fear that he isn't being completely honest with me."

"I'll be careful." I assured him. "Thank you for the warning."

CHAPTER SEVEN

The next day I got right to work with Simone, preparing the meal. Aimée was out in her herb garden. Henri was working on repairs around the house while Antoine and Jacques went hunting.

"I'm looking forward to this remarkable bread you have prepared," Simone said as I checked the Dutch oven. The scent of apple and cinnamon wafted through the air.

"I'm excited for you all to try it." I smiled.

"What is that Heavenly smell?" Henri entered the house.

"A special bread that Christine is baking." Simone smiled.

"Smells délicieux." Henri turned to me. "I've been thinking about what we can do in regards to Lewis."

"Perhaps we can…"

The door banged open, interrupting me. Antoine entered with Jacques hanging on him. A crimson stain bloomed across Jacques's shoulder.

"We were out hunting," Antoine said as Henri surged to his feet and went to help Antoine get Jacques to the bed. "I'm not even sure what happened." The young man ran a hand through his hair. "There must have been someone else out hunting. We separated and the next thing I knew, I heard a shot and Jacques crying out." Antoine looked panicked, sweat pouring down his face. Simone called out to Aimée, who quickly came in and gasped in horror at the sight of her husband, lying wounded on the bed.

"Jacques!" She exclaimed, then hastened to him and ripped his shirt open. The wound was gaping, and I had to turn away. "We must get you fixed up, mon amour."

"Not yet, Aimée, I must have time alone with Henri. Christine should stay as well." Jacques's voice sounded weaker with every passing moment.

"Jacques, you should save your strength," Henri protested.

"Not without saying what needs to be said." Jacques looked at Simone, Aimée and Antoine. "Please."

The three quietly did as Jacques asked. Henri had knelt next to the bed already, so I pulled up a chair to sit on the opposite side.

"What's so important, Jacques?" Henri asked.

"When I first found the key that brought me to the 1700's, I was in my element," he said. "I had always felt that I was born in the wrong century. Living more simply felt right to me."

"You've mentioned that," Henri said.

"I never wanted to go back to the 21st Century, and I firmly intended to live here until the day I died." Jacques struggled for a breath, then continued his story. "Unfortunately, I feel I may have made a terrible mistake years ago, just after Callum Lewis arrived. I didn't think anything of it at the time, but four years ago, Lewis found himself in a predicament. He was about to be killed by some Huron warriors and I stepped in and intervened."

"You saved that monster's life?" Henri asked, incredulous.

"Of course I did. I had no idea the kind of man he was, though I should have. Now, knowing of his plans, well, I'm afraid I may have allowed history to be forever altered."

I thought back to the books I had read that involved time travel. I had never considered the fact that it might actually be possible to alter history, but what Jacques said was very true. If Callum Lewis was supposed to die in 1772, but didn't, and his plot was carried out, if I made it back home, would it even be the place I knew and loved. Henri rubbed his head, as if contemplating the same thing. Jacques continued talking. "I suppose I broke the first rule of time travel by saving a man's life."

"You couldn't have known, Jacques." I placed a comforting hand on his shoulder.

"What else do you have to tell us, Jacques?" Henri asked.

"I've spoken to you often, Henri, about destiny and God's plan. I believe, and Aimée agrees, that you were brought here for a purpose. God put you at this time and in this place for a reason. I believe you are here to bring Lewis down, to fix my mistake. You are the perfect person to do such a thing, son, and I believe Christine was brought here to help you."

My heart pounded at his words. He couldn't possibly be serious. Then, I remembered my idea from earlier, about spying on Lewis and Hugo. I was so sure that I could help the people here. I always had visions of making a game-winning shot or hitting a walk-off home run, of being the hero. If I could muster up the courage, I could do so much more for this community.

"This makes my idea from yesterday even more of a necessity," I said to Henri. He simply clenched his jaw and shook his head.

"I do not want that," he interjected.

"We don't have much of a choice." I was surprised at my own bold words.

"You two will work well together," Jacques said, running his tongue over his cracked lips. "There is one other thing I must tell you before I pass on." He took a raspy breath. "I have had the key to get back this whole time. It has been in a small box under my bed, ever since I arrived here. I am sorry for being dishonest, Henri, but from the beginning, as I've said, I thought it was your destiny to be here. I know that I may have forever changed history and Mark's death will always be on my conscience, but if you and Christine don't defeat Lewis, the whole course of history could be, will be, altered." Jacques then closed his eyes, taking short, shallow breaths.

I placed a hand on Jacques's shoulder, but he seemed to have fallen asleep. "We'll talk things over Jacques, and we'll figure something out." I glanced at Henri, whose face was stone cold, his jaw clenched. He stood and stormed out. I gathered my skirts and followed him along the palisade walls to the lakeshore.

"Henri!" I called out to him. He stopped and turned, then ran his hand through his hair.

"All this time, the past three years…" He crossed his arms over his chest and looked out over the lake. "Jacques could have gotten us home at any time, yet he chose to lie to us."

"Henri, please…"

"No, Christine, you cannot possibly understand. Not only have I wasted three years of my life in the 18th Century, I lost my brother because of Jacques's dishonesty. He could have sent us back right away, but he didn't. If he had just let us go, Mark wouldn't have died."

"I know this is hard, but you don't know that for sure. Mark still may have died back home. Besides, what if Jacques is right and you're the only person who can stop Callum Lewis. What if it's your..."

"Please do not say destiny." Henri gave me a stern look, anger apparent in his voice. "I'm so sick of Jacques telling me about my destiny. I am not Harry Potter, no matter how often I've thought of Jacques as the Dumbledore in my life."

I wanted to smile at the pop culture reference.

"I just want to go home." Henri's voice went from anger to despondency. "I want to see my family, ride a Jet Ski, go to high school, catch a baseball, and get my driver's license. I've missed so many things."

"But you know as well as I do that the world we know and love may not even exist anymore if we don't somehow take care of Lewis."

"What would you have me do, Christine? Go and shoot him in the chest? Do you honestly think I haven't wanted to do that since he had my brother murdered? I find I cannot do that. Not only would I be caught and executed for even thinking about it, but I was raised to take the Ten Commandments seriously, and what I want to do to Lewis is definitely breaking the Fifth."

"I don't think we need to kill him, we just need to stop him." I replied softly, well aware that people could potentially hear our conversation.

"How do you propose we do that, Nancy Drew?"

I chewed on the inside of my lip, thinking. The idea had been forming in my mind since we had overheard Lewis and Remington. It was a daring plan, but I knew I could pull it off.

"I could go undercover."

"No." Henri turned away. With more boldness than I had ever mustered in my life, I grabbed his arm and pulled him to face me again.

"Henri, you have to see the wisdom in what Jacques says. I'm new to the area, no one really knows me. I could get close to the British soldiers, learn their secrets and weaknesses."

I could feel the tenseness in his arm. "Henri, I can get close to them. Maybe not Lewis himself, but Hugo or one of his other minions…"

"You're supposed to be my fiancée. How will you explain your lack of loyalty?" A small glimmer of hope welled up in me. Was Henri actually considering my idea? I didn't need his permission for anything, of course, but I wouldn't want to alienate him, the one person who was in the same predicament as me. We needed to work together if we were to get home.

"It's 1775 and I'm a woman," I replied. "I can pretend we have an arranged relationship, that I don't really want to marry and live with a fur trader, especially one who is continually getting into trouble with the brave, righteous British officers." With the last sentence, I took on a haughty, stuck-up tone in my voice, trying to convince both Henri and myself that I could pull this deception off. "They'll never think a woman could be so devious." I thought of all the famous female spies throughout history, women like Anna Strong of George Washington's Culper Ring, and Rose O'Neil Greenhow during the Civil War, just to name a couple. "I can do this, Henri, I know I can."

"I can't be responsible for another death, Christine, and I fear that Jacques's being shot was not an accident either." Henri's words were almost a growl. "This isn't some book or movie. You're not Hermione Granger."

"I am well aware of that fact, Henri, and I'm not trying to be a literary hero, but I must do something to get us back home. I've only been here for two days and I am already frustrated with the injustice I see here. I cannot imagine how you feel, being here for the past three years, how all the French traders must feel. The oppression has to stop, and if I can do anything to help, I will."

"Christine…"

"Besides, Mr. Beckwith, I may be known as your fiancée around here, but if I want to…" Henri clamped a hand over my mouth, quieting me.

"Alright," he said, then took his hand away. "I'm still hesitant for you to take this challenge, but you're right. Something must be done, and I couldn't stop you even if I wanted to." He shook his head. "Remington Hugo. He's your best bet. He has a weakness for the women here and isn't as smart as Lewis. He isn't completely dumb though, so you can't let your guard down." He sighed and rubbed his forehead. "I don't want to do this, but we should go back and speak with Jacques again. I can't believe he's known how to get home the whole time I've been here and has never told me."

"I don't know him terribly well, Henri, but he must have had his reasons."

"Yes, well, I'd like to know what they were," Henri replied.

"So let's go ask him." I persuaded Henri, knowing that Jacques could be of more help. "You know he also has more information that we'll need if we really are going to take on this mission."

Henri gave me a look that I couldn't quite decipher. "We," he finally said, "I have made some good friends here, but I've not really felt like part of a 'we' since my brother, Mark, died." He took a step closer and my pulse jumped. "How is it we barely know each other, yet you already know just what to say to me?"

I wasn't quite sure how to reply to that, so I just shrugged my shoulders. He took another step closer and placed a hand on my arm.

"Christine…" he leaned closer and I held my breath. Was he going to kiss me?

"Uncle Henri!" Rémy barreled into Henri, the impact throwing him into me. Henri's hands went around my waist to prevent me from falling.

"Rémy, be careful now." Henri reached down to pat the boy on the head.

"Papa is with Grand-père Jacques. You hafta come back to the house! He's hurt bad."

"All right." He turned to me. "May I escort you back to the house?"

"Yes, but if I act less than thrilled to be around you, know that I don't really mean it." I smiled.

He sighed. "I suppose we must start the illusion that you're not really happy with me."

"Remember, it's for the good of the entire mission." I whispered to him. He gave me another small smile.

"Of course."

We quickly made our way through the neighborhood and back to Jacques's home. Cort sat on a stump near the door, his face stoic, as I noticed he always was. Rémy went right to his father.

"What happened, Cort?" Henri asked.

"Jacques didn't make it," Cort replied.

My stomach lurched and I glanced at Henri, whose face turned ashen.

"That can't be possible." Henri pushed past Cort. Aimée sat at Jacques's bedside, and Simone stood at the fire, stirring the kettle, her red eyes the only sign of emotion. Jacques lay deathly still.

"Aimée, no. Cort can't possibly be right. How can Jacques be dead? He was fine when we left."

"The Lord decided it was his time," Aimée said.

"No!" Henri growled, anger apparent in his voice. "It can't be true. There was still much for us to say…" I could tell that Henri was trying to hold back tears.

"He told me to inform you not to worry about the last thing you said to him. He apologized again for not telling you everything. He told me to give you this." She handed Henri a key. I looked over his shoulder to examine it. The key looked similar to the one I still had in my pocket, only newer, not as rusted.

"He also said to tell you that he would not blame you if you left and took Christine and yourself home, yet he hoped you would stay."

"To fix his mistake." Henri muttered. I placed a hand on his arm in an effort to show my support.

"Henri, we can…"

He grabbed my hand and once again stormed out into the bright sunlight, this time away from the fort. When we were a safe distance away, he turned and placed the new key into my hand. I tried not to stare, but it looked as though he had tears in his eyes. The death of Jacques must have affected him more than he wanted to let on.

"Take it," he said. "Take it and get out of here. Go home."

"What?" I was stunned. If I took the key and left, how would Henri ever find his own way home? Besides…

"What about our plan? Henri, you just agreed that it was a good idea for me to learn exactly what Lewis is planning. I don't want to leave yet. I want to help." I folded my arms over my chest. "I won't leave 1775 without you, Henri."

He gave me an exasperated look. "I didn't realize you were this stubborn."

"I can be when the situation warrants it," I replied.

"And there's no way I can convince you otherwise?"

"No." I handed the key back to him. "When we go back, we go back together."

"I still wish you would change your mind," Henri said.

"I'm not going to, so just drop it." I shook my head. "I'm not afraid, I was born to do this." It was at that moment that I truly believed I was.

"Wasn't that a phrase used by Joan of Arc?" Henri asked.

"It was." I was pleased that he recognized it.

"All right. I am still not convinced that you should risk your life to help us, but I will trust you. Come on, if we're going to defeat Lewis, we should get to it."

"What's this about defeating Lewis?"

Henri and I turned to see Raphael.

"Raphael." Henri turned and acknowledged his friend. "I forgot to thank you yesterday. I understand it was you who got me out of that black hole so soon."

"Aye, it was nothing," he replied. "I was just at your house. I can't tell you how sorry I am about Jacques. He will be missed."

"You have no idea." Henri shook his head.

"I ask again, what are you two talking of? Do you truly have a plan to take down that scum of the earth?"

"Yes, Christine came up with an idea, at least some way we can start." Henri quickly told Raphael what I planned on doing.

"And you are willing to let your future wife risk herself like that?" Raphael asked. "I would never allow my wife to do so, even if I did believe she could help." Raphael turned to me. "Though if there was a woman here who could pull such a thing off, I am sure it would be you, Miss Belanger."

"Women have been able to do such things since the beginning of time, Raphael." Henri spoke up before I even had the chance. "Deborah was a fierce warrior-judge from the Bible, and Joan of Arc is a more recent example, then there is Molly Pitcher..." He trailed off as I looked at him in alarm. Molly Pitcher was a heroine of the American Revolution, someone who wasn't known to anyone outside her New England community.

"Of course, of course." Raphael held up his hands. "I want you to know that I'll do whatever it takes to help stop Callum Lewis as well."

60

"Yes, you do seem to have the ear of someone in the British Army," Henri said. His voice wasn't quite accusing, but I thought it a strange comment.

"I'm just a persuasive person." Raphael shrugged his shoulders.

"Well then, I'm glad you're at least on our side," Henri replied.

"Of course." Raphael slapped Henri on the back. "I'll even help spread the rumor that there is trouble between the two of you. I'd be willing to escort Miss Belanger around the fort in your stead."

"Yes, well, she's going to pretend I'm not good enough, so no offense, Raphael, but you wouldn't be either."

"I suppose, but I thought it wouldn't hurt to offer." He gave me a charming smile.

"Of course not." Henri shook his head again. "You do have that knack of always getting the ladies' attention."

"Well, it's hardly my fault they can't resist me, ami." Raphael laughed.

"All right then, gentlemen. I'll head back to the house and wait for an opportunity to speak with Hugo, you know, use what womanly wiles I can muster up."

CHAPTER EIGHT

I took a deep breath and walked towards Remington Hugo, nervous that he would stop me, yet knowing that he needed to do so in order for my plan to be set in motion. As I passed by, I gave the sergeant a quick glance. He caught my eye and gave me a grin that may have made my heart flutter if I didn't know what kind of man he truly was.

"Miss Belanger, I believe?" He stepped in front of me, blocking my way as I had suspected he would.

"Yes, sir, Sergeant Hugo." I gave him what I hoped was a coy smile. *You can do this.* I told myself.

"Where is your guard dog?" Hugo asked.

"Why, Sergeant Hugo, whatever do you mean? Are you in reference to Henri, my fiancée?" I gave him a dim-witted smile. "He's off, probably hunting or fishing. Whatever indelicate, unpolished men do."

"You're far too refined to be attached to a man like that."

"Why, thank you, Mister…I mean, Sergeant Hugo." I gave a short giggle, surprising myself with how well I was flirting with the man.

"It is my pleasure to say so. You let me know if there is anything I can do for you." He winked at me. My stomach felt a bit queasy. I didn't like being deceptive, even if it was for a good cause.

"I just might do that." I glanced over toward the neighborhood. "I must admit, I feel so much safer here, what with all of the soldiers about."

Hugo gave me another one of his smiles that just creeped me out. Could I do this? I had to. "We're here for the ladies, to protect you from all manner of boorish men." He looked up and I followed his gaze. An elegant-looking woman in her mid-thirties exited the commandant's house.

"My goodness Sergeant, is that Mrs. Rebecca DePeyster?" I reached out to grab his wool-clad sleeve. "I have heard so much about her. She is so elegant and her dancing, ooh lala! I heard she trained under a French dancing instructor in Edinburgh. I was so hoping to meet her. Could you..." I glanced at him, true excitement coursing through me. If I could become close with Rebecca DePeyster and earn her trust, I could appeal to her husband through her. "I don't suppose you could get me an introduction?"

Hugo puffed his chest and smiled cockily. "But of course I can, Miss Belanger." He offered his arm and I took it. We made our way towards the woman I had heard so much about through the years.

"Mrs. DePeyster, ma'am, how are you this fine day?" Hugo could turn on the charm when he wanted to.

"I am well, Sergeant, thank you." She smiled kindly.

"I would like to present you to Miss Christine Belanger, newly arrived from Montreal and engaged to one of the French traders who lives outside the fort, though I must say, I believe she is far too cultivated to be marrying the likes of any Frenchman."

I could feel my temper start to burn. Henri Beckwith was worth twenty Remington Hugos, yet the soldier treated him with such contempt. I had a role to play, however.

"Sergeant, such compliments." I tittered. "Mrs. DePeyster, it is such an honor. I have wanted to make your acquaintance since I heard you were here."

"My dear, you are too kind." She smiled, then looked at Hugo. "I suppose a young woman so accomplished could only help advance one of those rough French traders."

"She is not married yet, ma'am." Hugo looked me up and down again and I tried to refrain from shuddering. "There's still time."

"I assume you plan on being married by Fr. Gibault." Mrs. DePeyster addressed me.

"Of course, that is the plan," I replied with a glance at Hugo. "Although I must admit, there have been many times when I question the wisdom in following through with the marriage." I hoped I sounded convincing.

"Well, my dear, this sounds like something that should be discussed in more detail over tea. I was just on my way to visit my dear friend, Archange Askin. No offense intended, we usually don't associate with the French, but we may be able to make an exception for today."

My heart pounded, almost not believing my luck. Tea with Rebecca DePeyster? Getting the information and contacts I needed had been easier than I had anticipated.

"It would be my pleasure, Mrs. DePeyster. Thank you."

When I returned to Jacques's home in the late afternoon, Henri all but grabbed me and dragged me back outside.

"Well?" He asked, exasperated. "What did you learn?"

"I'm learning right now that you're impatient." I pulled away from him and put my hands on my hips. "Can you give me a moment to breathe?"

"My apologies. I've spent the better part of the day speaking with Fr. Gibault about the funeral for Jacques. I'm sorry if I want to get this situation taken care of posthaste."

I immediately felt bad for snapping at Henri.

"And I'm sorry for yelling at you just now." Henri rubbed his head. "I just...now that going home is in my grasp, I want to go more than ever. But I know I must finish my business here."

"I understand, and I'm sorry too. I know how anxious you must be." I paused. "When will the funeral be?"

"Tomorrow. He'll be laid to rest then." Henri shook his head. "I cannot fathom Aimée's pain. Burying her second husband." He sighed. "Jacques upset me so much yesterday, and I still feel betrayed by his lie, but he was a good man. The best kind of man. He rescued me and Mark when we first arrived here, and was kind and understanding through so much..." He paused.

"He was like a father to you." I finished his thought.

"For the past three years, yes." Henri admitted. He looked somber, almost like a little boy, and I wanted to pull him into my arms and comfort him.

"I'm sorry, Henri." The words felt inadequate.

"Well, I suppose the only thing we can do is make it alright by getting rid of Callum Lewis," Henri said. "I don't know why, but I have a gut feeling that he's somehow responsible for what happened to Jacques."

"I thought Antoine said it was an accident."

"He said that, but he also admitted that he didn't really know what happened."

"Why would Callum Lewis want to have Jacques killed?"

"I'm not sure, exactly, but Jacques was a leading member of the French community and he's raising metis children as well as me, and I've been a thorn in his pretentious side since I got here."

"I suppose." I shook my head, hoping Henri was wrong and there hadn't been a murder. "Perhaps I can find out more from my new friends."

"Yes, of course, we got distracted," Henri said. "What did you learn?"

"It's not so much what I learned, but who I met." I quickly told him about my conversation with Hugo and tea with Mrs. DePeyster and Mrs. Askin. "Again, I didn't learn much, but I laid quite a bit of groundwork. If I can get the ear of the Major's wife, I will be well-placed to earn her trust and that would only help our cause."

"Probably, but." Henri sat down on a log. "I must say again, I do not like you socializing with Remington Hugo. The man's a womanizing letch, and I know exactly what he's after from you."

I blushed, knowing Henri was right. "I'll be careful, I promise."

Henri just grunted. I shook my head and sat next to him. "Henri, don't worry. I'm not the naïve colonial Lewis thinks I am. I'll be just fine."

"I can't have anything happen to you," he said. He opened his mouth to speak again when Simone peaked her head out the door.

"Henri, Christine, dinner is ready." She spoke softly, then went back inside.

"How is everyone holding up?" I asked Henri, feeling guilty. I had been so excited at the progress I had made with the British that I had forgotten about Jacques's family and their suffering.

"As well as can be expected, I suppose." He stood. "Aimée and Simone will be taken care of, even with Jacques gone. Cort and Antoine will make sure of that, and Raphael has a good relationship with Aimée." He took my arm and escorted me in. "Come on. Maybe venison stew will make things better."

CHAPTER NINE

Over the next few days, I pretended to grow more distant from Henri and his family while spending more time with the British. In reality, I found myself wanting to spend all my time with Henri. He appeared gruff and grumpy, but I could tell he was also kind and caring and very protective of his family.

Jacques's funeral had gone as well as could be expected. Though Père Gibault hadn't known Jacques well, he gave a very moving eulogy. Aimée had cried, as did Simone. Cort was as stoic as ever, and Antoine was silent almost the whole day. Remy stayed close to Aimée, which I hoped was comforting to her.

"Miss Christine." Remington Hugo's voice came from behind me. Simone and I were doing laundry for the family. Simone gave him a wary look, then glanced at me disappointedly. I wished I could tell her why I was being so friendly with the British, but I couldn't risk her knowing.

"I have a few free hours," Hugo continued. "Would you care to go for a stroll with me?"

I didn't want to, not really, but I hadn't been able to get much information from Hugo yet, despite spending time with him on a daily basis.

"That would be very nice." I wiped my wet hands on my apron. "I just need to freshen up inside."

"Of course," Hugo said. Simone followed me inside.

"What are you thinking?" Simone grabbed my arm and pulled me around. "Going for a stroll with Remington Hugo is like walking with the devil himself." This anger was very uncharacteristic of the calm Simone I had gotten to know. "Now I know you and Henri are up to something. You cannot deny that. And I trust Henri explicitly, but you cannot risk walking outside the palisade walls with that soldier." She bent close. "He's evil, Christine." Her voice shook and it made me wonder, not for the first time, if Hugo had at one point forced his attentions on her. The young woman seemed positively terrified of him.

"I appreciate your concern, Simone, but I am wise to him. I assure you, I will be just fine." I took off my apron and brushed off my skirt. Simone shook her head.

"Christine, please…please be careful."

"I will, I promise. I'll be back before supper." I then quickly left to join Hugo.

"You must forgive my tardiness, Sergeant. Simone was trying to convince me to stay away from you, though for the life of me, I cannot understand why. My only thought is that she is concerned for Henri's welfare, though I have made it clear I have no interest in marriage to him. My only other thought is that she's jealous of the attention you're giving me." I hated gushing over this man, who I knew was simply power-hungry. Whenever I was with him, he was haughty and cruel to anyone beneath him.

Hugo chuckled and pulled a flask out of his haversack, then took a swig from it. I wasn't an expert on the different scents of alcohol, but I would guess he was drinking rum. If alcohol made him talk, this walk could work even more in my favor.

"I just wish I could find some way, you know, some reason to break my betrothal. Alas, my parents insist upon it. Jacques was a dear family friend, and they have been planning this marriage for years."

"Evans is dead now, an' if all goes as planned, Beckwith may not be long in this village either."

My heart pounded. Could this be a moment of truth? I gripped Hugo's arm as we walked farther from the safety of the fort. "Why, whatever do you mean, Sergeant? Do you have an idea for me to avoid marriage to that man?" *Play ditzy, play ditzy.* I reminded myself.

"I'd support you right now, Miss Belanger. Keep you in comfort. In exchange for a special friendship, of course."

I felt nauseous just thinking about what he was suggesting, but I pretended to be dense.

"I do appreciate your friendship, Sergeant Hugo, but please tell me more of this plan you have to rid me of Henri Beckwith."

He took another drink of rum. I wondered if he was becoming intoxicated. "No' my plan. Leftenant Lewis's plan." He grinned saucily and pulled me to a stop. I glanced back at the fort. The palisade walls were more than 100 yards away, and we were just inside the tree line. I felt my heart hammering in my chest. Perhaps this had been a stupid idea. He gripped my forearms. I tried to remain calm. "I'll tell you all about the plan in exchange for a kiss."

I forced a smile on my face. I didn't want to kiss a man like this, but if it would help me discover the plan...

I reached up and teasingly kissed him on his cheek.

"I must tell you, I don't usually give my kisses away so freely." I hoped my voice was light and teasing. Hugo frowned.

"Guess I should earn it, then."

I backed away a step as he took another swig of rum.

"Lewis is the smartest man I know. Not sure why, but he plans on ridding this fort and the entire straits area of all the French and those with any French blood. He knew Jacques Evans was a French leader 'round these parts, so he was the first to go."

I tried not to withhold a gasp. Henri had been right. Jacques was murdered.

"Lewis, he has someone on the inside learning all about the French and any plans they may have. Someone not even Jacques suspected." Hugo took another drink.

"What is Lewis...I mean, how does Lewis plan on accomplishing this feat? Won't Major DePeyster suspect something?"

"Whal, yer beau is the next to go. Thet won't concern DePeyster. Beckwith's always been a troublemaker, he and that brother of his. It'll be easy to convince the major that Beckwith deserved to die. After that, Lewis actually..." Hugo bent down, conspiratorially. "Lewis has a plan fer DePeyster, too. Trouble is brewin' back east. Durn colonials and their little rebellion has the major on edge. Lewis convinced 'im to personally go out an' talk wit' our injin allies. Then, when DePeyster comes back..." Hugo pantomimed drawing back the string of a bow and shooting an arrow. "'E'll meet an end that'll look just like a meti' piece o' dung kilt 'im. They'll blame them stinking half breeds."

71

I couldn't believe my luck. I had done it, I had uncovered Lewis's plot, yet it was worse than I had imagined. "Just call me Nancy Wake," I said to myself, referencing the heroine of World War II who was active in the French Resistance movement, smuggling messages and food to underground groups in Southern France and helping refugees flee to Spain.

"So ye see, ya don' haveta worry 'bout Beckwith. 'E'll be gone, then ye can be mine." He stepped forward, grabbed my arms again, and roughly pulled me to him. Before I could protest, he kissed me. I shoved at him with all my strength, but he would not budge. "Don't ye be fightin' me now." He shoved me to the ground and all but fell on top of me. I tried not to panic and maneuvered my body so I could get a little bit of space. Finally, I saw an opportunity and threw my knee into his groin. He fell back slightly, which gave me the opportunity to push him away. Heart pounding, I turned to escape, but ran smack into another solid body.

"Christine!"

I breathed a sigh of relief when I realized it was Henri. He steadied me, then stormed toward Hugo, who was pushing himself up.

"You no-good son of a..." With as much force as possible, Henri punched Hugo, then took him to the ground. Hugo tried to fight him off, but Henri's anger, combined with Hugo's tipsiness made it difficult for the soldier. Henri continued to punch Hugo with a ferocity that almost scared me. I rushed to the men.

"Henri, come away." I grabbed his arm. "Come on!" I couldn't allow Henri to be arrested when I had just learned the information that we needed. Hugo was almost unconscious and hopefully wouldn't even remember telling me what he had. I gave Henri's arm a tug and finally pulled him away.

"You'll pay for this, Beckwith, mark my words," Hugo muttered, then turned over and lay face down.

Henri turned to me with unabashed emotion, and pulled me into a tight hug. "Please tell me you're alright."

"I was more scared than anything, but I was able to fight him off. Luckily, he had been drinking, so it was easier to get away."

"Thank goodness Simone found me. What were you thinking, going off with him like that?" Henri started pulling me towards the Evans home.

"You know darn well, I escaped that pain in the rear all on my own," I said. "I knew I could get some information out of him and oh, did I. Henri, Hugo all but admitted that Lewis had Jacques killed."

"I knew it! I just knew it," Henri growled. "How?"

"Hugo made it sound like Lewis has a man on the inside, someone in the French community that is spying for him. I didn't find out who, but Henri," I pulled him to a stop, needing him to fully understand what I was going to say next. "Henri, he told me that you are next. They want you out of the picture, just as they wanted Jacques out of the way. Lewis wants to destroy all the French and metis. Not even Hugo knows why."

"Hugo just wants to throw his power around, he wouldn't care about specifics." Henri ran a hand through his hair. "I want to kill him for abusing you like he did, for even thinking he could put his hands on you."

I was touched by Henri's words. They sounded quite gruff, but I could sense an undertone of caring. We continued walking."

"But I'm all right. We will get through this, Henri, I promise." I smiled. "I have faith."

He tried not to scoff, but I could tell he wanted to. "I'm glad one of us does."

"I thought you mentioned attending church. At St. Anne's, on the island…"

"That may be true, Christine, but I've been having a difficult time believing that God has a hand in any of this."

I was taken slightly aback. "Very well, Henri, but I want you to know that I'll be praying for you."

"If you want to waste your time with that, then I'm not going to stop you."

We neared the Evans home. It was almost time for dinner. We had extra fish soup for the midday meal, so we would be having leftovers.

"You could still go home. Right now," he said. "You've accomplished your mission, you've discovered Lewis's plot."

"That's partly true," I said "but my mission isn't quite finished. I plan on helping you, all the way through to the end." I slid my hand down his arm and squeezed his hand. "Unless you really want me to leave." I surprised myself with the flirty, playful words. Henri pulled me to a stop and faced me.

73

"I don't want you to leave. I only want to protect you, yet I know I can't do this without you." He pulled me closer.

"Henri," I whispered, desperately hoping that my instincts were right and he was going to kiss me. He leaned down and I closed my eyes...

"Henri Beckwith, you are under arrest."

My eyes flew open. Two British soldiers grabbed Henri and pulled him away. Callum Lewis stood just behind them.

"On what grounds this time?" Henri pulled at their hold.

"The attack and attempted murder of one of His Majesty's Soldiers." Lewis replied.

"That is not what happened." I protested. "Mr. Beckwith was only protecting my honor!"

"That's not what our witness said, and the witness is one of your own," Lewis replied.

"You can't do this!" I panicked. This had to be the next step in Lewis's plan. Kill Henri and get him out of the way.

"We most certainly can," Lewis said. "And if you're not careful, Miss Belanger, I'll have you in chains as well."

"Christine, don't!" Henri cried. "I'll be fine, don't worry."

"Rest assured, Leftenant Lewis, I will be speaking with Mrs. DePeyster about this and you know how much she has her husband's ear."

"I might be concerned about that, except for the small fact that the Commandant just left to try and work out a treaty between the Fox and the Chippewa Indian tribes. He won't be back for at least a fortnight." He motioned to his soldiers. "You know where to bring him." The two soldiers dragged him away toward the land gate of the fort.

"Find Benedict Arnold, Christine," Henri called out. "We need to find him."

It took me a moment to process what he was saying. Benedict Arnold, the most infamous American traitor. Henri wanted me to find the person in the French community who was betraying their people. No one here would know who the actual Benedict Arnold was, though he was alive right now. George Washington, Benjamin Franklin...all of our founding fathers were alive. I shook my head. "Focus on the task at hand, Christine." I told myself. I couldn't dwell on meeting American heroes when Henri and the others needed my help.

"What just happened?" Simone came out of the house, followed by Aimée and Antoine.

"Henri was just arrested again." I quickly explained what had happened, watching their expressions. I hated thinking that one of them could be the traitor, but it could be anyone. Simone had sent Henri out to find me, knowing he would defend me by attacking Hugo. Could she have been setting Henri up? Antoine was with Jacques when he was shot, could he know more than he let on? The snitch could even be Raphael. Henri had made some comments that pointed suspicion toward the voyageur. How could I help Henri when I had no idea who I could trust?

"I'll go find Cort," Antoine said. "He might have an idea on how we can get him out."

"Come, Simone," Aimée said as Antoine jogged off. "I know the Leftenant has a soft spot for you. Perhaps we can go speak with him and convince him to release Henri."

Simone nodded, though she looked nervous at the thought.

I wasn't exactly sure what I should do next, but before I could decide, Raphael ran up to the house.

"Miss Belanger! Thank goodness I caught you." He was winded, as if he had run all the way here from his voyageur encampment. "I just heard what happened to Henri. Are you all right?"

"How did you hear about Henri's arrest already?" I asked him, ignoring the question.

"It may not seem like it now, with all of the traders and voyageurs here, but we are a relatively small community, Miss Belanger. Now, I repeat, are you all right?"

"I have had better days," I admitted, then told him where the other family members had gone. "I assume Henri is in the black hole again? Do you think we can see him again?"

"No, not yet. They're aiming to make a public example of him. He's to get twenty lashes."

"They're going to whip him?" I had never understood the phrase 'my heart stopped' until that moment. "No. How can they do that without a trial?"

"Lewis already ordered it, and DePeyster left him in charge. He can justify it by claiming that he's keeping the peace."

"I have to go to him! Oh, when is this debacle to take place?"

75

The bell from Ste. Anne's Church rang. Raphael looked in that direction. "It sounds like right now."

"Right now? How can they do that? Don't they need to talk to the other witnesses, like me?" My stomach clenched.

"They're British soldiers, Miss Belanger, they can do with us what they wish." Raphael looked at me as though he couldn't believe I was questioning the power of the British. I never understood the Founding Fathers and Patriots fighting the British more than I did right then and there.

I hiked up my skirts and sprinted towards the fort. Soldiers, traders and Indians were already gathering near the guardhouse. I pushed my way through the crowd. "Oh, Lord, please, no."

Henri had his hands tied up high on the pillar outside of the guardhouse. Aimée and Simone stood in front of Leftenant Lewis, pleading with him. As I went to join them, two British soldiers pushed them back into the crowd. Lewis nodded at another soldier who held a whip in his hand. The man reached up and tore Henri's shirt, baring his back. Then Lewis spoke to the crowd.

"This man, Henri Beckwith has been found guilty of assault on one of his majesty's officers. He may also be guilty of attempted murder or even murder of that same officer. Until that is determined however, he will receive punishment for assault and blatant disrespect. Let this serve as a reminder to you all. Insubordination will not be tolerated."

"I tried to reason with him, I really did." Simone approached me, eyes red. "That man is mad."

I took a shaky breath.

"Twenty lashes," Lewis commanded. The soldier with the whip raised his arm and cracked it against Henri's back. He jumped in pain and a red mark immediately formed. Henri groaned. I stepped forward, wanting to go to him.

CRACK! Another lash, this one drawing blood. I bit my lip. Tears fell down Simone's cheek and I noticed a tear falling down the face of the usually-stoic Aimée. On the seventh lash, Henri let out a yelp of pain. Four lashes later, he groaned, then appeared to pass out. The soldier raised his arm to whip Henri again.

"No!" I cried out, then tried to run up to Henri. I wasn't quite sure what I would do once I got to him, but I couldn't just stand there and watch. Before I took two steps toward him, Raphael grabbed me by the waist and held me back.

76

"It won't do him any good and it will just make things worse for you." He whispered to me.

"They're killing him." I practically moaned.

"He's strong, that one. Henri will be just fine."

I turned and clung to Raphael, burying my head in his shoulder. He patted my back. I just couldn't watch any more, but closing my eyes didn't stop the horrifying sounds of that cracking whip.

CHAPTER TEN

After the whipping was over, two soldiers dragged the unconscious Henri into the guardhouse and left him on the floor near the black hole.

Raphael continued to pat my back gently. "Come, I'll talk to the guards to see if they'll let you clean him up." He moved and spoke to one of the soldiers, Sergeant Logan McIntosh. The man glanced at Lewis's retreating back as he headed toward the commandant's house, then nodded. Raphael approached me, Aimée and Simone. "Sergeant McIntosh said you can tend to his wounds. While you do that, I will ask some questions of the soldiers. Henri is still a prisoner but we have to find a way to get him free. I have no doubt that Lewis will look for any excuse to execute him."

"I'll go get some ointment and rags for those wounds," Aimée said. "Simone, we'll need some fresh water."

Simone nodded and followed Aimée. I made my way up the stairs and into the guardhouse. I couldn't help but gasp when I saw Henri's mutilated back. It was all I could do not to throw up. I quickly walked to him and knelt down. Not wanting to touch his back before Aimée had a chance to clean it, I reached up and pulled a sheet from the guard's bunk, balled it up and carefully placed the sheet under Henri's head for a pillow. Though I tried not to wake him, he stirred and groaned, but kept his eyes closed.

I brushed back his hair, hoping to comfort him. "Oh, Henri," I murmured. "We must end this before you get yourself killed."

He groaned again, then moved his hand to take hold of mine. Before I could say anything else, Aimée and Simone both arrived. As they cleaned and bandaged his back, I kept hold of his hand, offering whatever help and comfort I could. When they had done their best to clean him up, Aimée put a new shirt on him that she had brought from their home. Finally, Henri squeezed my hand with a bit more strength and let out a moan.

"Aie, my back. That hurts like the devil."

"Rest up, Henri. Save your strength." Aimée told him.

"If Callum Lewis has his way, it won't matter how rested I am." Henri muttered. He focused his eyes on me. "Did you find Arnold?"

"I haven't had any time to investigate, I'm afraid." I replied. "But I will start immediately."

He nodded. Raphael poked his head into the guardhouse. "Lewis and some men are on their way over here. We'd best leave."

Aimée kissed Henri's forehead and followed Simone and I out of the guardhouse. Sergeant McIntosh nodded briefly at us as we left, then we started walking to the Evans home.

Aimée shook her head. "Mon Dieu, first Mark, then Jacques, now Henri. Help us, Lord."

"Don't worry, Tante Aimée," Raphael said. "Cort and Antoine will be at your home by the time we get there. I have some information and an idea on how to get Henri out." He took my arm in his. "We'll get him out, Mademoiselle Belanger, worry not."

"I want to help," I told him. "I must be able to help you somehow."

"Of course, of course." Raphael replied. "You have already proven yourself quite capable. If Henri trusts you, then I can do no less."

Relief coursed through me. "Thank you." We approached the Evans home. Cort sat out front on a log and rose when he saw us coming.

"I heard what happened. Antoine didn't reach me fast enough." He shook his head. "Henri really stepped into a mess this time." He glared at me, as if knowing it was my fault.

At that moment I realized just how much it was my fault. I had thought I could handle myself with Hugo, but my actions had caused Henri to be arrested and now possibly executed.

"I'm sorry, I wasn't thinking..."

"This is not your fault, Christine." Simone defended me and glared at her brother. "You cannot blame her for the mistakes of other white women, Cort. She is only here to help."

I glanced at Cort, whose jaw tightened even more, if that was possible.

"Passing blame won't do Henri any good." Antoine entered the conversation, coming from around the corner of the house. "We need a plan and we must all work together."

"I have an idea," Raphael said.

"What are you thinking?" Simone asked. "Out with it, we must act quickly if we are to save Henri. We are all willing to help."

"I know you are," Raphael answered. "For right now, however, I'll just need Cort and Miss Belanger. The rest of you, lay low. My idea may need more assistance."

"If it's not a good plan, then why use it?" Cort asked. At the same time, Antoine spoke up.

"What about me? Surely I'm more valuable than Christine."

I bristled and was about to defend myself when I realized what time period I was in. Almost everyone felt the same way about women that Antoine did.

"She has skills that I believe we can use to our advantage." Raphael said. I wasn't sure what those were, but I did not want to be left out of saving Henri.

"Come on, then," Cort said. "We need to hurry. There's no telling what Lewis is going to do next.

"Unfortunately, I do know, and it does not bode well for Henri," Raphael said. "I was able to find out that Lewis doesn't want to risk an execution. DePeyster wouldn't allow it without having his say, but Lewis wants Henri gone by morning. He's keeping him in the powder magazine and not the guardhouse, citing the need for extra protection, as if that makes any sense. The building isn't usually guarded, but Lewis has posted one there now. That's where you come in, Christine." He nodded at me. "I have the keys to his shackles, so..."

"Where in the world did you get…?" Cort interrupted, but his question was cut short by Raphael.

"I have my ways, and it's best you don't know." He nodded at me. "We need you to talk with the guard, he's easily distracted by a pretty face. Cort and I will slip in and get Henri out. That way, when Lewis sets fire to the magazine…"

"He's going to what?!" I tried to keep my voice down. "Lewis is going to blow Henri up?"

"He's darn well going to try, but we won't allow it." Raphael said. "After we get him out, we can bring him to his own land and keep him there indefinitely until we can figure out another plan."

"Well, let's focus on Henri's escape, then we can worry about the next step. The important thing is getting Henri out before he's blown up," I said, still in disbelief that even Lewis would do something that dastardly.

"Precisely," Raphael said.

"All right, then, it's getting close to sunset," Cort urged. "We need to move quickly."

Just as we entered the fort through the back land gate, two British soldiers approached us.

"Raphael Lafontaine and Cort Lefevre, you are both wanted for questioning by Leftenant Callum Lewis. Come with us now."

"We will find you as soon as we are able," Raphael said to me. Cort looked like he wanted to argue, but thought better of it. Raphael took my hand in his, passing something small and metallic into my palm. He then brought my hand to his lips and made a show of kissing it. "Until then, Mademoiselle."

Cort and Raphael followed the soldiers as I fingered what Raphael had given me. A small key, just the right size for shackles. I took a deep breath. Cort and Raphael being brought in for questioning was no coincidence. Lewis constantly seemed one step ahead of us. How was he able to continually do this? Who was his inside man?

I sighed and thought about how I could get Henri out on my own. The area around the powder magazine was clear of men and campsites, as no one wanted to build a fire too close to the explosive material and risk a spark. As I studied the fresh-faced soldier who stood guard, an idea formed in my mind. I took a deep breath, then moved to the alleyway between the magazine and the palisade wall. Glancing around, I quickly found a rock, then focused on what I needed to do and prayed for courage.

"Help!" I screeched. "Oh, dear, I need help, please!"

As expected, the guard dashed around the corner. With a swing of my arm, I smashed the rock into his head. He staggered, but didn't fall. In desperation, I grabbed the musket from his hand, pulled back and slammed the musket against his head. He fell unconscious. I hurriedly pulled the keys to the powder magazine from his belt and hastened to the door.

The powder magazine basement was one of the only structures that had survived to modern times, so it was slightly familiar to me. I looked around the dark room. There wasn't as much powder and ammunition as I would have imagined. Perhaps Lewis had pulled some out, knowing it would be destroyed when he set fire to the building.

"Henri, where are you?" I called out quietly, wishing I had brought a lantern. "Oh, hang it." I pulled out my phone and clicked on the flashlight. I only had 50% battery life left, but I had to find Henri.

"Christine, what…" I heard his weak voice call out from the corner and rushed over to him. His face was covered with cuts and bruises. It appeared as though Lewis and his men had beaten Henri after the whipping.

"We need to get you out of here." I quickly unlocked his shackles. "I'll explain everything I can later." I put his arm around my shoulder to help him stand, then assisted him to the door. Just as we were about to make a clean getaway, the soldier I had knocked unconscious stepped in front of us. Henri pushed me behind him.

"You." Though the soldier seemed dizzy, he punched Henri, throwing both of us back into the magazine. He then slammed the door.

"I don't think he even saw you," Henri groaned, rolling over. I bit my lip when I saw some of the wounds on his back were bleeding through the binding.

"Henri, we need to get out of here. Lewis plans on setting fire to this building, with you trapped inside as a prisoner."

Henri's face went white. "And now you'll be killed too. How stupid can I be." He stood as quickly as he could. "The back trapdoor, do you remember it? I'm not even sure if Lewis knows about it. Come on."

Again, he had to lean on me for support. I couldn't help but panic a bit when I smelled smoke coming from the doorway. The fire had been lit. I let Henri lead the way to the second exit of the magazine. I wasn't as confident as he was that it would be a good escape route, but we had no other options. We reached the trapdoor, in a corner right above our heads. I was relieved to see it latched from the inside.

"Let me boost you up so you can open it." Henri gripped my waist and mustered up the strength to lift me as I braced myself against the wall and reached up toward the latch. I could feel heat from the fire and the smoke was making it difficult to breathe. We had to hurry.

My sweaty fingers slipped on the latch, but I finally got it open and threw the trapdoor up. I flinched, expecting to see a musket pointed at me, but no one was in the vicinity. Thankfully, it was getting dark. I did hear cries of the people.

"Fire!"

"The powder magazine!"

"Stay back, it'll blow!"

"Get out!" I felt Henri's hand on my bottom as he frantically shoved me up. I gripped the sides and hoisted myself up and out of the basement. My heart thudded when I saw that the building overtop the magazine was burning quickly. I reached down to help Henri. He gripped my hands and I pulled with all my strength. Henri groaned and cleared the hole, his momentum carrying him into me. We both fell backwards, him on top of me. I pushed Henri off, rolled over and pushed the trap door shut.

"Come on, we have to go," I said. Henri groaned. I helped him up and, not letting go of his hand, pulled him to the palisade wall. We continued to walk along the wall, keeping to the shadows.

"It's going to blow!" Someone in the crowd yelled, and then, seconds later, an explosion rocked the ground. The force from behind threw both Henri and me to the ground again. Dirt dug into my palms and Henri's body landed on mine once again, shielding me from the explosion.

"Are you all right?" He asked, his voice right in my ear.

"Yes, are you?" I glanced over at him. "I do wish you would stop falling on me, though. I am not a pillow."

"I'll work on that. Let's get out of here." He struggled to his feet once again and pulled me up this time, then leaned on me as we made our way along the wall. As we exited the land gate, I braved a look behind me. Angry orange flames consumed the wood building as another explosion rocked the ground. A crowd was gathering, though everyone was keeping their distance.

The distraction was a welcome for me and Henri as we slipped outside the fort and headed west.

"We can't go to Jacques's, but I know of a place where we can hide," Henri told me.

I let Henri lead the way while I half-carried him. He was still so terribly weak, especially now that the adrenaline of nearly being blown up had worn off. We stumbled along for what felt like hours. I was surprised and impressed with myself for not passing out, but I had my mission and was determined to complete it.

"It's not that much further." Henri was breathing heavily and moving slower. I had to get him to rest soon. The full moon was shining brightly and reflected off the big lake, giving us just enough light to see by, though we kept to the edge of the woods for protection. Finally we turned into the woods when I saw a small, one-room dwelling that wasn't quite finished.

"Henri, what is this place?" I asked as he opened the door to the unfurnished room.

"It's mine." He groaned as I helped him to sit down on the dirt floor. "Jacques was helping me build it. No one else knows about it though, so we should be relatively safe."

"It's very nice, I looked out the glassless windows across Lake Michigan. "Such a beautiful location. You should actually purchase the land now. You could make a fortune from the property when we get back to the future."

"Not sure it would work that way." Henri smiled a rare smile. "But it is a nice spot. We're about a mile past McGulpin Point." He found the stored lantern, lit it, and sat back on the floor.

"That's good to know." I sat down on the floor next to him, then looked up. He had yet to construct the roof, so I could see the stars through the trees. "It's so peaceful out here. Hard to believe all the destruction that's happening not far away." I turned towards him. He had closed his eyes and was leaning his head against the wall. I touched his arm. "How are you feeling?"

"Like I was hit by a semi-truck." He opened his eyes and looked at me. "And so glad I have someone who understands that reference."

I smiled and looked down at our hands. Henri had taken mine in his and shifted his fingers so they were between mine.

"Is there anything I can do for you?" I asked.

"Just stay with me," he replied. "I don't want you going back to the Evans home tonight. It's too dangerous. You can head back in the morning. Get some supplies." He squeezed my hand. "And tell no one where I am. Pretend I'm dead, that you weren't able to get me out. The only person I fully trust right now is Aimée, but I don't want her to risk coming out here."

"There is no one else you trust?" I asked. "Cort and Raphael were ready to break you out of the magazine, but Lewis had them brought in for questioning, and Antoine and Simone were both ready to do whatever it took to release you."

"I believe with my heart that Cort is trustworthy, and Simone doesn't have a devious bone in her body. Antoine is young and so eager to be a man, I'm just not sure anymore, and Raphael..." Henri shook his head. "He seems to have an ear in the British camp, he's always in the know."

"I can't imagine Raphael would..."

"Christine, may I ask who came up with the plan to get me out? Who even discovered that I was being held in the magazine and not the black hole?"

"It was Raphael, That's true, but..."

"Exactly. He always knows..." Henri ran a hand through his hair, something I noticed he did often. Sometime between his whipping and now, he had lost the strap holding his hair back, so his hair hung down and brushed his shoulders, making him look even more attractive.

"Perhaps you should ask him…"

"Yes, and I am so sure that he would admit it," Henri said sarcastically. "Just like Benedict Arnold would have admitted his plan to give up West Point if George Washington had asked him about it."

"Hmm." I looked up again. "Crazy how that hasn't even happened yet."

He nodded. "I know, right? Our revolution is happening right now and yet we're over here, just trying to survive.

I was glad he had calmed down. I hated thinking that anyone from Jacques's family was the traitor, and I truly didn't believe it was Raphael.

"This snitch, do you have any idea who else it could be? Not someone from your family, but others in the area?" I realized that I really hadn't met that many people in the French community.

"I don't know. Maybe." Henri rubbed his forehead, smearing a bit of blood.

"We need to get you cleaned up," I said, examining his face. "And your back. How does that feel?"

"Like I fell on a thousand shards of glass," he replied. "Though I suppose I should be thankful to you, Simone and Aimée for patching me up."

"I didn't do much," I admitted.

"I knew you were there the whole time. Your encouraging words and touch were very soothing. It helped immensely."

"I am glad to hear that." I smiled. Henri leaned forward.

"Christine, I…" He reached forward and touched my cheek gently. "I never wanted you to be put in the middle of all this." His voice was low, his lips inches from mine. "But I must admit, I can't see myself doing this with anyone else." He finally closed the distance between us and kissed me. He moved to pull me closer, and I gently pushed him away.

"Christine…" He pulled me in to kiss me again, but I leaned back. I wanted to kiss him back, but with our isolation and the chemistry zinging between us, I knew I had to keep my distance.

"Henri, that was…I…" I stood and took a deep breath, then leaned against the wall.

"I'm sorry, Christine. I thought you…well…" He ran a hand through his hair again.

"It's not that I don't want to kiss you. I do." I paused, unsure of what to say next. "I'm just...not the kind of girl to...you know." Dylan Rodriguez's words popped into my brain. "In fact, I must admit, I really haven't been kissed much. I know that may sound unusual, but..."

Henri shook his head and struggled to stand. "Christine, I am not about to judge you for that, just the opposite, in fact. I'm glad you're not that kind of girl." He approached me and held my hands. "It makes me feel special. Now, to make a confession." He smiled again. "That was my first real kiss. I'm not counting Marla Summers in the second grade."

His words warmed my heart.

"I feel like I've been waiting for you my whole life, mon petite amie," he said. I knew Henri wasn't one for flowery words, but those ones touched my heart.

"That's a sweet thought," I said. "And I'm glad you will understand when I sleep on the opposite side of the room tonight."

"I will insist on it." Henri assured me. "But I do want you to know that you can trust me."

"I do know that," I replied. "If I didn't, I probably would already be back at the Evans's."

"Smart girl." He gently lowered himself back down to a sitting position. "It's time to get some sleep anyways. We need to figure out what we're going to do next and we will need fresh minds to do so in the morning."

"Yes, that's true." I crossed the room. "Sleep well. I'll see you bright and early."

CHAPTER ELEVEN

The next couple of days fell into an uneasy routine. I worked with the Evans family for long hours, and I would also go out to check on Henri. I told the family that I needed some time to think and pray for my fiancé. I was able to bring him food, medicine and news. I kept my eyes and ears open, desperately looking for evidence on who the turncoat was.

Three days after the powder magazine explosion, as I was walking around the corner of the fort to get water for Aimée, a familiar British soldier stopped me.

"Sergeant Hugo." I tried to mask my fear with happiness. "It is ever so wonderful to see you, and looking so well." I had heard he was better, and that he believed a skewed version of what happened: Henri had attacked him after Hugo had brought me to the Evans's house. It seemed that, time and time again, I was forgotten or unseen, an effect of being a woman in the 1770's.

The soldier who had set the magazine on fire insisted that Henri had attacked him and had been acting alone. I wasn't sure if that was what he truly believed or if he knew he had been knocked out by a woman and didn't want to admit it. At any rate, the rumor was that Henri had died in the explosion and I had nothing to do with any of the events.

Aimée and her family were devastated, and I longed to tell them that Henri was alive, but we had agreed that wouldn't be for the best. There was to be a funeral service for Henri tomorrow.

"I am so happy to see you, Miss Belanger." Sergeant Hugo smiled as if he hadn't forced himself on me. I tried to control my breathing as he stepped closer. He had almost overpowered me once. Would he try to do so again? "I wanted to make sure you were okay. You were likely distraught when you discovered that your intended was still alive."

"What?" My face drained of color. How did Hugo know that Henri was still alive?

"I am sorry for distressing you, Miss Belanger, I assumed you'd heard."

At least he thought my shock came from the news itself and not the fact that he knew. "Are you positive, Sergeant? How is this possible? How do you know?"

"One of the Frenchmen informed me. Not sure how the frog found out, but Lewis is taking the information seriously." The bells of Ste. Anne's church chimed. "In fact, that's likely Lewis making the announcement now." Hugo held out an arm to escort me in. I took it reluctantly.

"What announcement?" I asked.

"You'll see." Hugo led me to the front of the crowd gathered at the commandant's porch. Callum Lewis stood there, looking as menacing as possible. When it appeared everyone from the fort and village had assembled, he held up a hand. I saw Raphael on the other side of the crowd and he locked eyes with me, concern on his face, as it had been for the past two days. He felt responsible for Henri's supposed death and had been trying to make it up to me. I shook my head at him and smiled, hoping he understood that I needed him to stay away.

"We have been informed that the French trader, Henri Beckwith is still alive." Murmurs through the crowd could be heard. "We also have knowledge that he is responsible for the fire that caused the powder magazine to explode."

"No," I whispered, though the accusation shouldn't have surprised me.

"Beckwith is at large, but we believe he is still in the area and is a threat to our community. We have learned that Beckwith has a plot concocted with other members of the French community, including the now deceased Jacques Evans, to take over Michilimackinac. If anyone has any information on the co-conspirators or where Beckwith may be, you are by law required to share that information."

My heart pounded. How had it come to this? He was accusing Jacques and Henri of treason, a crime that's punishment was death.

"If anyone withholds information, the penalty could be your own death." His eyes darted around, resting briefly on Raphael, Aimée, Cort and Simone. I looked around for Antoine, but didn't see him. "Finally, all know this: there will be a reward for bringing Beckwith in, be it alive or dead. The soldiers of the King's 8th Regiment have been ordered to shoot him on sight."

I couldn't contain my gasp. Why couldn't Lewis just let things go? Unfortunately, I knew the answer: he was pure evil and perhaps he realized that Henri wouldn't rest until Lewis was stopped.

"No reason for you to worry, Miss Belanger." Hugo patted my hand as if to comfort me.

"My goodness, this is all so much to take in. I cannot believe this! Oh, I must be going." I released his arm. "I almost forgot the water I was fetching. I'd best finish my chores and allow you to get back to your duty."

"Of course. I would like you to know that it would be my pleasure to personally be the one to bring Beckwith to justice."

"I am sure you are the right man for the job." I nodded. "Good luck, Sergeant." I backed away and carefully made my way back to the buckets I had abandoned earlier, walked back to the lake to fill them up, then brought them back to the Evans home. I couldn't understand how the British had discovered that Henri was still alive.

When I arrived back at the house, Aimée was working on the meal and Simone was in the back garden.

"Here's the water," I said. Aimée nodded somberly. I glanced out the window to make sure Simone couldn't hear, though I was positive she wasn't the traitor. "And worry not, Aimée. I have a feeling Henri will be just fine."

"You knew he was alive the whole time, didn't you?"

I spun around to see Simone in the doorway, hands on her hips.

"Yes, I did," I admitted. "And I wanted to tell you, but Henri insisted I tell no one."

"I should have guessed." Simone shook her head. "How could you keep this from us? How could you let us grieve once again for another loved one? I believed us to be friends, Christine."

"It wasn't my choice, Simone, and we are friends, but we didn't want anyone to get into trouble. If you were questioned by the soldiers, you could have honestly said you didn't know anything. Me, I could be arrested right now for what I know."

"That is where you ran off to every day," Aimée commented. "I must admit, I hoped that's what you were doing."

I was once again grateful for Aimée's quiet, steadfast trust.

"When you go next time, you must take protection." Aimée went to the corner and pulled out a musket and bag that I assumed held rounds and powder. "And leave it with him so he can defend himself."

"Of course," I smiled, "I was planning on going berry hunting today."

"Good, I'd like to go with you." Simone insisted.

"That's really not necessary," I protested.

"Do you even know how to fire that musket?" She asked.

"As a matter of fact, I do," I replied, glad for the soldiers I worked with at the fort taking a morning to hold 'musket day' with the female interpreters, teaching them to load and fire. "Please, Simone, believe me. Henri will be fine, but the more people who know his whereabouts, the more at risk he is."

"She is right, my dear," Aimée said. "It is best if you stay. Trust Christine and trust that God will watch over them both." She handed me some comfrey and bandages.

I nodded, glad that Aimée understood.

"Can she at least take Cort with her?" Simone asked.

"Henri insisted. No one." I stood my ground.

"All right then." Simone said, though she didn't sound happy about it at all. I nodded, then threw the musket over my shoulder, gathered a bucket for the pretense of berry picking, and left to check on Henri and give him the new information.

"But how did they find out? Were you followed?" As expected, Henri was not happy when I told him that Lewis had discovered he was alive.

"No, I don't think so," I replied. "I was always more than careful coming out here, doubling back, wandering, never taking the same path more than once."

"It has to be the spy, somehow, but how would they..." He clenched his teeth. "Well, I suppose since they haven't captured me yet, they don't know where I am."

"They wouldn't have found a body, perhaps they figured it out that way."

"Perhaps." Henri paced back and forth. "I can't keep lying low like this, Christine. I have to get out of here, I have to do something."

I looked around the room. "You could probably try and spruce the place up a bit. Make it more habitable."

The comment got me a patronizing smile with a hint of annoyance. "Thanks, but the nearest Walmart is twenty minutes and almost 250 years away."

"It was just a suggestion." I smiled back. "I do understand, though. I definitely wouldn't want you to get hurt trying to put the roof on or drawing attention to yourself by chopping down a tree."

"Exactly." Henri muttered. I could tell he was still in pain, but at least being bored had given him an opportunity to recover.

"How are you feeling? Really?" I asked. "Aimée sent me some supplies so I can check your wounds and replace bandages."

"I'm fine as far as I can tell," he said. "I'd like for you to check my back, though. I can't tell what it looks like and there are some areas that still hurt quite a bit."

"After twenty lashes, I'm not surprised." I muttered. "All right, then, off with your shirt."

"I thought you weren't that kind of girl." Henri winked and I blushed, enjoying the fact that we could banter, but also because I was getting a fluttering feeling in my heart at the knowledge that I would have to rub the homemade salve over the bare back of the boy I was attracted to.

Henri reached down and pulled his shirt over his head, then turned so I could see his back. I took off the bandages and I couldn't hold back a gasp."

"Please tell me that's a 'goodness that's a nice looking back', not a 'gross how disgusting is that back' gasp."

I tentatively placed a hand on his shoulder. "It's an 'I'm so sorry for the pain you've had to go through' and 'I can't believe you're not in a constant state of tears' gasp."

"So it's that bad?"

I looked at his back again, crisscrossed with angry red marks. Many of the wounds were still open and draining.

"It's not good, that's for sure," I replied, as I got to work cleaning the wounds, then dabbing the comfrey on the deeper cuts. I wrapped the new bandages firmly around his torso and turned Henri around.

"Thank you." He pulled on his shirt. "That feels much better."

"I hope I'm not interrupting anything." A voice said from the open doorway. Henri and I spun around to see Raphael.

"How? How did you find me?" Henri glared at Raphael, frustration evident in his voice.

"I followed Miss Belanger, of course, the day after the explosion," he stated. "She didn't make it easy, I'll give her credit for that, but you must remember my father is one of the best trackers in the straits area, and my mother's people are well-known for those same skills all over this so-called French North America. I doubt anyone else could have followed her, so you shouldn't worry about that. What you should worry about is…"

Henri took a step towards Raphael. "I think I should be worried about my closest friend betraying me over and over again." Henri burst out. "You've been telling one of the Redcoats everything, haven't you? How else are you always the first to know everything and are always one step ahead of our moves?"

"I've told you before, I'm just persuasive."

"That's not it and you know it!" Henri shouted. "How else would Lewis know I'm alive in addition to all of the other information he learns? Not to mention the fact that Remington Hugo told Christine that Lewis has a man on the inside."

"I know he does, Henri, but that man isn't me. I am trying to protect you. That's why I'm here now. Whoever is feeding the information to Lewis found out where you are and now he's gathering a small contingent to come and get you as we speak. We need a new place for you to hide, now."

I grabbed Henri's arm. "Henri, we need to listen to him. The soldiers have been given orders to shoot you on sight."

94

Henri tightened his jaw, looking like he wanted to punch something.

"I don't know…"

Raphael jumped back against the wall and motioned to Henri and me to do the same.

"Someone's out there," Raphael whispered. "Henri, you get ready to move. Christine and I will distract them."

"How will we do that?" I whispered back.

"Of course you will," Henri muttered, but he still picked up the musket I brought and moved to the back corner where he had cut out a hole for a window and jumped out.

Raphael moved in front of me. "Just play along," he whispered, then kept an eye on the door. When the first Redcoat barged into the room, Raphael lowered his head and kissed me. My initial reaction was to push him away, then I remembered that we were a distraction, so I placed a hand on Raphael's back and prayed that Henri got away. *Please help him get away, Lord.*

After a second, Raphael pulled away, pretending surprise at being caught and gave the soldiers, who had filed into the house a sheepish grin. I gasped and covered my mouth, recognizing a few of the soldiers.

"Uhh, hello, gents." Raphael pulled away from me. "To what do we owe this visit?"

"We're tracking Beckwith." Sergeant Logan McIntosh shouldered his musket. "Thought he might be hiding out here."

"Ahh, well, I've been out here every day since my canoe came in." Raphael replied. He gave me a sly glance. "If Henri had been hiding here, I'm uhh…sure he would have made his presence known."

"I'd assume so as well, and it would be unlikely you'd survive that confrontation, Lafontaine." McIntosh said.

"Indeed." Raphael chuckled nervously. I blushed, embarrassed by what the soldiers all thought I was meeting Raphael for.

"Well then, we'll let Leftenant Lewis know that his informant was mistaken." McIntosh nodded and touched the brim of his tricorn hat. "Ma'am."

"Sergeant McIntosh." I nodded back. After they left, I punched Raphael's shoulder. "What was that all about?" He knew I was referring to the kiss.

95

"My apologies, mon cher," he said. "Just remember, it was for a worthy cause, and it worked."

"I suppose, but you didn't have to be so convincing," I said, "and I must remind you that I am not the type of lady who gives her kisses away willy-nilly."

"Willy-nilly?" Raphael gave me a confused smile.

"To just anyone." I clarified. "So that will not happen again." I shook my head.

"Of course," Raphael said. "I can respect that."

"Good," I replied, then turned toward the window Henri had jumped out of. He was long gone. "I wonder where he went."

"I have an idea or two. I can track him later." Raphael exuded confidence.

"I suppose I'll head back to the village. I'd still like to find out who is giving Lewis the information."

"You don't believe it's me?" Raphael asked. "Henri seems convinced."

"I don't know what to think anymore, and I'm not sure he does either," I replied. "It won't hurt for me to do some more recon."

"Recon?"

"Information-finding," I replied. "Come, let's go."

CHAPTER TWELVE

The next day, Raphael came to see me.

"I tracked Henri and know where he is hiding. Worry not, he'll be safe."

"Can you take me to see him?" I was anxious to check on him and make sure he was all right. I needed to keep him updated on everything that was going on.

"I'll take you out there a little later," Raphael assured me. "We must be careful, especially now that rumors about the two of us have spread."

"What?" My mouth dropped. "You and me? You mean that we..." My face got red. What must these colonists think of me? Engaged to one man, spending time strolling with a British soldier and now sneaking off to meet a third man.

"It's a small community. It was bound to happen, and it does give you a good excuse for leaving the fort so often. Most will assume you were meeting me and not think that you were caring for Henri."

"Oh, my reputation is in shatters." I buried my face in my hands.

"Perhaps, but we need to find a way to stop Lewis. Once we do that, we can work on repairing your reputation."

"Once we do that, I'm going home," I groaned.

"If that's what you want."

"Christine, there you are." Antoine came around the corner. "You're needed at the commandant's house. Mrs. DePeyster has requested your presence."

"Good grief, whatever for?" I asked.

"Not sure, but I can escort you," Antoine took my arm. Raphael narrowed his eyes at Antoine, almost in a warning not to try anything with me. I wanted to roll my eyes. I had always wondered what it would be like to be popular. I suppose now, with all these soldiers and traders and voyageurs vying for my attention, I was getting a taste of it.

"Thank you, Antoine." We walked into the fort and quickly made our way towards the commandant's house.

"So do you believe what Lewis is saying?" Antoine asked. "About Henri, and him blowing up the powder magazine?"

"Not at all," I replied. "You shouldn't believe it either. He's been like a brother to you for the past three years. You should know he wouldn't do that."

"I suppose, though there has always been something different about Henri. Some of the things he says and does. What if he's been planning something like this the whole time?"

"You cannot possibly believe that," I replied. "You know him better than that."

"I must say, I find it hard to believe how much trust you have in him right now. It seems to me that it didn't take you long to switch your loyalties from Henri to Remington Hugo, and now Raphael, as it turns out."

I blushed. "I've had very little experience in socializing with men," I admitted. "Coming here, well, marriage is a big step. I want to make sure Henri is right for me."

"It doesn't matter what you want," Antoine argued, taking a typical colonial stance on marriage. "You don't have a choice. Your parents and Jacques made an agreement. Henri is your betrothed. That's as binding as being married." Antoine seemed angry, obviously feeling a fierce loyalty to Henri. Then why did it sound as though he doubted Henri's intentions? "I suppose I should be well aware that you women from Montreal don't view marriage and commitment the way you should."

His words confused me. That hadn't been the first time that one of the Lefevres had made a comment about 'women from Montreal'. Before I could ask Antoine any further questions, we arrived at the commandant's house.

"Welcome, Miss Belanger." Sergeant Logan McIntosh was guarding the door. "Mrs. DePeyster wanted you to wait for her in the parlor. She'll be back directly."

"Thank you." I nodded to both McIntosh and Antoine, then walked into the empty parlor. Just opposite from me was the commandant's office. I glanced towards McIntosh, who was shutting the door and could no longer see me. I quietly crept toward the desk, thinking maybe I could find some information to exonerate Henri and implicate Callum Lewis. With the 'Mission Impossible' theme song running through my head, I silently rifled through some papers.

"Hmm." When I came across some documents that seemed suspicious, I took a closer look. I was no accountant or bookkeeper, but one of my sisters had taught me the basics. Something definitely looked out of order. I pulled out my phone. I was down to 43% battery, but I still had my charge stick stashed in my pocket. "At least I don't have to worry about roaming." I muttered, then I pressed the screen to get to my camera app and snapped some pictures. Perhaps Henri and I could work together and figure out if my suspicions were correct. I pocketed my phone, looked at one more document, then turned to head back into the parlor and jumped when I saw a soldier in the doorway. My heart almost stopped when I recognized Callum Lewis.

"I wondered if you would take the bait, and you did not disappoint." His voice was deadly calm, yet at the same time, menacing.

"Why, Leftenant Lewis, I have no idea what you are talking about." I tried to act unaffected and flighty, but I could tell that Lewis wasn't buying it.

"Don't play innocent with me, Miss Belanger. I've known since you arrived here that there is more to you than meets the eye. Though I cannot quite put my finger on what it is."

"I'm afraid you're mistaken, sir. I just came to visit with Mrs. DePeyster, who requested that I wait for her in the parlor. Since it was empty, I simply began wandering around. Nothing dastardly, I assure you." I took two steps toward the doorway, hoping to push past him. My heart pounded furiously. As I neared him, he grabbed my arm and threw me against the wall, then caged me in with an arm on each side of my head.

"Rebecca DePeyster is at the Askin's. She doesn't wish to socialize with you. Why ever would she? You are the fiancée of a stinking French fur trader, and, what's worse, you give your favors to other men."

"In spite of what you've heard, that's not..."

"I care not about your morals, Miss Belanger, I care about the information you will give me in regards to Henri Beckwith. I know he's alive. I know you helped him escape. I know you're privy to his whereabouts now."

"You're partly right," I admitted. "I may have known where he was right after the fire and explosion, but God as my witness, I do not know where he is now." Terror shot through me at the anger in Leftenant Lewis's eyes.

"I am not some simpering sot, Miss Belanger." He grabbed my arm and pain shot through me. He gave me a quick shake. "You will tell me or I will give you to Sergeant Hugo and allow him to get the information from you his way."

I took a deep breath and tried not to panic as I fought to push Leftenant Lewis away. If I could just get free for a second, I could make a break for it.

"Leftenant Lewis..." the voice at the door distracted the evil officer enough for me to bring my knee up between his legs. Lewis doubled over in pain, but retained a tight hold on me. Mustering all my strength and courage, I thrust the heel of my hand into his nose. He yelled out again and released me. I shoved away from him and ran past the interrupting soldier, hoping he wouldn't stop me. Instead, he put a hand on my back and helped me along.

"Come out back." It was Sergeant McIntosh. He led me out the back and through Mrs. DePeyster's garden, then out the watergate. Waiting there was an anxious-looking Raphael.

"It was as I suspected," McIntosh said. "We need to get her out of here." He shook his head. "I cannot go back either, as I have been found out."

"Blast it all." Raphael started to hurry along with us in the same direction as Henri's house was. "I'll show you where to go, then head back and see if I can learn anything."

I was confused at this new development, the trust Raphael put in Sergeant Logan McIntosh, but I had to put my own trust in Raphael. I didn't have any other choice.

Back in the fort, the bells of Ste. Anne's rang loudly.

"That's Lewis again. No doubt making sure everyone knows Miss Christine Belanger and I are now wanted as well." Sergeant McIntosh said.

"Why did you help me?" I panted as we made it to the tree line, where we could finally slow down. I was in good shape, but most of the running I did was in shorts and a t-shirt, not long skirts, a shirtwaist and stays.

Raphael glanced at McIntosh. "We might as well just admit it now."

"I suppose," McIntosh replied. "Go ahead."

"You and Henri, have been questioning me on how I know so much about the British and how I can get such reliable and quick information." Raphael said. "McIntosh here has been my source all along."

"Again, why would you help the French? You're British."

"Scottish, actually, but I am a British soldier, true. That's doesn't mean I approve of all they do." McIntosh replied. "I respect DePeyster, he's a good man, but Lewis and Hugo…I could not let them get away with what they were doing any longer. No decent human would."

"I'd agree with that," I said.

"I've also developed a liking for Miss Simone Lefevre." McIntosh said. "I couldn't let anything happen to her or anyone in her family. I have failed at that quest with the death of her stepfather, I can't fail again."

"We have to band together and stop the madness," Raphael said. "Enough is enough."

"My sentiments as well." McIntosh said as we rounded a bend. "Outlaws rising up against an evil leader. Not unlike the story of Robin Hood."

"I'm not sure who that is," Raphael said. "But it sounds like a worthy story."

"It is," I agreed. "When will we reach Henri?"

"Not far now," Raphael told us. About twenty minutes later, he stopped and made a bird call. Henri appeared from behind a tree, musket gripped in his hand. He nodded, and we followed him around a dense bend down into a rocky ravine. I looked around the area. It was very rough, with a fire pit and a small lean-to built of pine boughs and branches. Staying here would be considered very rustic camping.

"I was hoping it was you, Raphael," Henri said suspiciously with his musket loaded and ready to fire, "but why did you bring a Redcoat?"

"Because he saved your woman from the clutches of Callum Lewis, that's why."

"And he's the reason Raphael knows so much about what's going on at the fort. Sergeant McIntosh wants to help us." I added.

Henri hesitated. I stepped forward and touched his arm. "Please, Henri. It's time for you to be a little more trusting."

Henri clenched his jaw and grunted what sounded like 'fine.' Then he turned to me.

"And what, may I ask, did Raphael mean about saving you from Lewis?" He reached out to take my hand.

"I don't know how, but Lewis knew I helped you escape. He set a trap for me and I, like a ninny, fell for it. Now I will be just as wanted as you are," I replied. "And since Sergeant McIntosh helped me, he is most likely a wanted man as well."

The sergeant nodded. "Although I do wish I had known she could take care of herself beforehand. I wouldn't have had the need to expose myself. She knew just what to do to take down Lewis."

Henri looked at me proudly.

"Just call me Lara Croft, Tomb Raider." I added.

"So I'll leave you three here. I'm going to speak with Cort and Antoine to see if they have any ideas on what to do next." Raphael said.

"Remember, we still don't know who's feeding Lewis information." Henri ran a hand through his hair. I was beginning to like that habit of his. "Whoever it is must have known that Christine is still loyal to me." He squeezed my hand. "Who is this culprit that is always a step ahead of us?"

"Whomever it is, they're good." I shook my head. "Aimée and Simone know that I was only pretending to enjoy the company of Hugo Remington, and I trust them implicitly. There's no way Simone would go to Remington or Lewis, she's pretty scared of the British soldiers."

102

"With good reason, based on what I've heard," McIntosh said. "If her brother knew what happened to her, he wouldn't be so chummy with any of the soldiers."

Raphael, Henri and I looked at McIntosh at the same time. "What do you mean?" Henri asked, confusion apparent in his face. "What brother? Surely not Cort."

"No, the younger one. I've seen him conversing with Lewis himself a time or two. It never really coincided with anything in regards to you, Beckwith, but now I'm wondering if maybe he's the one you're looking for."

"Antoine?" Henri shook his head. "That can't be. He's just a kid."

"Just telling you what I saw." McIntosh shrugged his shoulders.

"I agree that it makes no sense, but lately, nothing does. I'll look into this and see if I can find anything out," Raphael said. "But no, I find it hard to believe that its Antoine. He's not deceptive enough."

"He is the one who brought me to the Commandant's home under false pretense," I said thoughtfully. "I assumed a soldier had told him to bring me to Lewis, but perhaps I was wrong."

"Well, let us know what you learn." Henri nodded at Raphael, who nodded back, then turned to leave.

"Be careful!" I called out. He waved and started to jog back towards the fort.

"What I wouldn't give for some cell phone service right now," Henri whispered so that only I could hear. That reminded me of the pictures I took.

"I have something to show you." I gripped Henri's arm. "Sergeant McIntosh, would you excuse us for just a moment?" I asked.

"Of course." He nodded, then sat down on one of the logs.

Henri and I moved to a spot, looking out over Lake Michigan. From what I could tell, we were now just east of McGulpin Point.

"What is it?" Henri asked. I pulled out my phone and pulled up the pictures I had taken.

"I found these papers on the commandant's desk." I showed him. "I'm not exactly sure, but I believe it shows that someone has been...embezzling. Not money, though. Guns and ammunition. Someone must be selling them and pocketing the money."

"No wonder the magazine was emptier than I would have expected." Henri flipped through the pictures.

"That's exactly what I thought."

"These papers make it appear that DePeyster is the one behind the stealing, but that doesn't make sense. He's way too honorable."

"But Lewis is not. Remember, he means to kill DePeyster, perhaps he is setting him up as well. If the major is dead, he would never be able to prove his innocence."

Henri nodded. "That makes sense. Lewis wants wealth, power, and prestige and he can get all of that here."

"I realize that, but what is his motivation, why is he willing to hurt so many people?" I bit my lip.

"He's just pure evil, Christine, like those Unsubs that the BAU can profile on Criminal Minds. Lewis is worse, so much worse."

"Perhaps you're right."

"Come, it's getting close to dinner. All I have is hardtack and jerky, but it will have to do. We can talk over your findings with McIntosh. I don't think there's much we can do about it now, but it is definitely something we can use later."

CHAPTER THIRTEEN

It was two days before Raphael came back. Henri was going stir crazy. I was lucky to have the calming presence of Sergeant Logan McIntosh, who balanced out Henri's edginess quite nicely.

"Raphael! What news do you have?" Henri asked. The voyageur looked pale and once he got closer, I noticed that his face had several bruises.

"Raphael, what happened?" I reached up and touched his shiner.

"British soldiers, what else?" He explained. "But that's not important. Lewis is tired of waiting for the British soldiers or the citizens in the village to find you. He's getting you to come to him."

"Don't tell me he's taken someone hostage." Henri scoffed.

"Not sure what that means, but he is holding Tante Aimée and Simone. Says he'll give you three days to turn yourself in. No shot's fired. If you don't, he says he'll have them both executed."

"What?!" Henri shouted. "On what grounds?"

"Withholding evidence, conspiracy, Lewis doesn't need much of a reason anymore. With DePeyster gone, he thinks he can do whatever he wishes."

"He really must be stopped, and now." Henri started in the direction of the fort. I quickly darted in front of him and placed my hands on his chest as if I could stop him.

"You cannot go off all half-cocked like this, Henri Beckwith." I scolded him. "All that will accomplish is you getting yourself killed. Now settle down, we need a plan."

He clenched his jaw. "And I suppose you have one."

"Not quite yet, but if the four of us put our heads together, we can surely figure something out."

Henri turned to McIntosh. "Can we trust you to risk your life? I know Raphael has family ties to Aimée and Simone, but if you throw in with us, you could be killed."

"This may sound dramatic, but I would die a thousand deaths for Simone Lefevre." McIntosh spoke calmly and confidently. I couldn't help but smile at Sergeant McIntosh's passionate declaration. I hoped he would get a chance to tell Simone his feelings. She deserved some happiness like that in her life.

"All right," Henri said, sounding slightly surprised by McIntosh's admission. "Let's put together a plan."

"I know I don't have any good ideas, but I'm not so sure about this plan." I mumbled as we made our way back towards the fort. Raphael and McIntosh had already gone ahead, setting the plan into motion. "We still don't even know who the traitor is."

"We are all aware of that, but we don't have enough time to worry." Henri whispered back. "I just pray it's not Raphael or Cort or Antoine or anyone else that Raphael recruited to help with this plan."

"At this point, with everything Raphael has done, I hardly think he's the one who is working against us."

"I really want to believe that, I do." Henri grabbed my arm and pulled me to a stop right before we emerged from the tree line. "Christine, there is one thing I need to tell you before...if this doesn't work out..." He slid his hand down to mine. "If something happens to me, you mustn't think twice. You have to take the key and get out of here as quickly as possible."

"I will," I promised and patted the pocket of my borrowed trousers where it was being kept safe. I had dressed in men's clothes, as it would be easier for me to move. "Don't worry though, Henri. God will see us through."

"I hope He does," Henri said. "I also need you to know that...I care about you a great deal. If we were back home, I'd ask you to be my girlfriend."

I smiled at him. "Well, when we get out of this mess, you can be my date at the Homecoming dance."

"I'll hold you to that." He bent down and kissed me. "It's a good incentive to get out of this alive."

I gushed inwardly at his words. He really could be romantic when he wanted to be, and it felt more genuine than all of Raphael's flirting. He looked out across the land between the tree line and the fort.

"One more thing, Christine. Just in case I don't make it and you go back alone. Will you find my parents and somehow put their minds at rest? Tell them that Mark and I will never make it home."

I nodded. "If that does happen, I'll let them know that both you and Mark died heroes."

"Thank you." He smiled. All right then, let's get to it."

The plan was simple, but it was a simpler time, so hopefully, it would work. We hastened across the field. My heart was racing and from the breaths Henri was taking, he was feeling the same way. He still wasn't completely healed.

We crept around the outside of the palisade wall, then peeked around the corner, waiting for Raphael's signal that everything was in place. Henri continued to hold my hand, which gave me a great deal of comfort.

Please, Lord, help us make this work. I closed my eyes and prayed. Henri gave my hand a squeeze.

"Say one for me, too." He whispered.

"I have been," I assured him.

"There's Raphael." Henri nodded. "It's time." He pulled me close and hugged me, hopefully not for the last time. We then separated and I made my way to the water gate.

It didn't take long for a crowd to gather when the people noticed Henri making his way from the land gate to the commandant's house. I snuck through the watergate once the British soldier guarding it moved inside. I crept along the king's storehouse and waited. I noticed Sergeant Logan McIntosh across the path from me, using the garden fence of the commandant's backyard as a shield. Raphael had brought him civilian clothes, so

107

he looked very different. I crept closer to the commandant's house where the crowd had gathered in front of the parade grounds. I strained to hear what was being said. Thank goodness Lewis had been true to his word and no one had shot Henri as he walked in.

"I'm here, Lewis. Now let the innocent women go."

Not for the first time, I wondered where Rebecca DePeyster was and what she thought of this whole ordeal.

Two British soldiers immediately grabbed Henri and checked him for weapons, then quickly put shackles on his wrists. "You have me, where are Aimée and Simone?" Henri repeated.

"They're safe, you can trust me. You must believe me when I say I would never allow harm to come to Miss Lefevre."

"So you say," Henri retorted.

Lewis waved his hand in the direction of the guardhouse and two privates brought Aimée and Simone out of the building and past the parade ground to the front of the commandant's house.

"Henri!" Simone called out.

He smiled weakly at them. I sent up a silent prayer of thanks that they were safe. So far, our plan was working.

"So now what, Lewis. You have me here. What's the next part of your plan?" Henri had to be careful not to taunt Lewis too much. He had the crowd as witnesses.

"I believe you need some discipline before you are tried for your crimes. However, clearly, the standard whipping last time didn't have a deep enough impact."

My heart raced as they led him towards the guardhouse again. I looked toward the land gate and saw two villagers close it. Another part of our plan clicked into place.

"I believe it should be the knout this time," Lewis said.

"No!" I gasped. Callum Lewis was truly a sick-minded individual who drew pleasure from torturing people. I knew that a knout was a type of whip with rawhide thongs attached to the handle. Rumor around the village was that Lewis had metal shards and hooks attached to his. If our plan didn't go right, this punishment would kill Henri.

I gulped down some bile in my mouth and glanced towards the roof of the guardhouse. Two of Raphael's men should be up there, ready for the next part of the plan.

Lewis's men unshackled Henri so they could wrap his arms around the post of the guardhouse. This was it. Raphael sneaked up to Aimée and Simone and spoke low in their ears. Just as the British were about to tie Henri up, I saw Cort crouched on the roof with Antoine just above him. I held my breath, waiting for them to jump and tackle the soldiers. Instead of staying low, however, I saw Antoine straighten up.

"What are you doing, stay low." I whispered, as if the boy could hear me.

Lewis's eyes looked to both men on the roof. Without warning, Antoine threw his weight against his brother. Cort fell from the roof, hitting his shoulder hard on the ground.

Henri used the distraction to knock one of the soldiers next to him away. Raphael pushed forward as the villagers began to shuffle around. Henri helped Cort stand, then, pulled a club from Cort's belt and hit Lewis, who was poised to attack Henri. Things were happening fast, and not according to plan. One of the soldiers pulled a pistol out and fired at Henri as he, Raphael, Cort, Simone and a few others raced toward the water gate. That was my cue. I quickly moved to one of the doors of the gate as McIntosh moved to the other. When I turned around, I frowned when I saw Aimée, limp in Cort's arms. As soon as my team was through the gate, along with the villagers who were helping us, McIntosh and I pushed the gates closed. Once they slammed shut, McIntosh snapped the padlock in place and we all ran for the trees. The British were locked inside the fort for now, but they would find a way out soon enough. I heard them stomping up the stairs to the catwalk.

We were halfway to the tree line when shots began ringing out.

"Keep going!" Raphael yelled. The Redcoats reloaded, then shot at us again. This time, I felt something graze my arm. It stung, but I pushed myself to run harder. I was so glad Raphael had brought me the men's breeches and a shirt. It was so much easier to move.

We finally made it to the tree line, where we could slow down. I was able to look around and take attendance of who had come out with us. Simone, Cort, Aimée, still in Cort's arms, Raphael, Logan McIntosh, Henri, and about a half-dozen Frenchmen that I recognized, but didn't know their names. Henri made his way to my side and took my hand.

"We must keep moving," Raphael said. "Henri and I have a new location to hide at. We should be safe there."

"For now," Henri groaned, then sighed and looked around. "Wait, did we leave Antoine? Where is he?"

"We did not leave him," Cort said, his jaw clenched. I was terribly impressed by Cort's strength, as he was still carrying his mother with a shoulder that I was fairly sure he had dislocated. Henri stopped.

"Then where is he?"

I squeezed Henri's hand. "We'll talk about it when we get to camp." I told him.

"He was Lewis's inside man, wasn't he?" Understanding dawned on Henri, who still didn't move. I waved the rest of the group ahead.

"Yes, he was," I said softly. "He and Cort were on the roof. Antoine stood to let Lewis see him, as a warning I would guess, then intentionally pushed Cort off the roof. It was all the warning Lewis needed. It's what messed up the plan. Not too badly, though."

"I wondered how Cort ended up on the ground like that." Henri looked ahead. "And in the confusion, Aimée was shot. We came to save her and she ended up with a bullet in her anyways."

"It's not your fault." I told him, knowing that he would be blaming himself.

He took a deep breath. "And now, we must figure out what to do next. At least we know who the traitor is. Antoine. This whole time, it was him. His family must be heartbroken, he's just a kid. I cannot believe it." He began walking quickly again. "I feel so stupid for not realizing it. I mean, I knew that it could be him, I just didn't actually think it would be, you know."

"Yes, I understand," I replied. "There may have been some minor indications, but it's when you look back and put all the signs together that it makes more sense."

"I suppose." Dusk was falling as we turned into the woods to follow the rest of the group. We're going to have to alter our plans. Learn when DePeyster is coming back. It's our only hope of defeating Lewis for good. If we can somehow show the major those pictures you took or better yet, the actual documents...that might sway things in our favor."

"I hope so, but we need to stop Lewis from killing DePeyster first."

110

"I have been thinking on that. I'm hoping that Sergeant McIntosh might have more information, and we still have Cort and Raphael, Michael and the others to help, of course."

I was glad to see that Henri was finally learning to trust.

"Who is Michael?" I asked, reminded that there were a half-dozen men on our team that I didn't know.

"Raphael's father. One of the best tracker's I have ever met. I think we can try yet again to devise a good plan with who we have here."

"That's promising." We finally caught up with the rest of the group. Cort still carried Aimée, who remained unconscious. It worried me. Should we have bandaged her wound already? My own injury seemed to pale in comparison to what she must be feeling.

Henri pulled me around and touched the cut on my arm. "I saw this earlier and thought it was just a scratch. Why didn't you tell me you were shot?"

"It's just a flesh wound. I'll be fine. I'm more worried about Aimée." I brushed his hand away. "How much longer until we reach the new camp?"

"It's not far." Henri assured me. I could tell he was still bothered by Antoine's actions. I was as well.

We finally reached our destination. As we arrived, Rémy jumped up and raced to his father.

"What happened to Grand-mère?" The boy asked.

I noticed a woman in her mid-thirties stand and walk to one of the Frenchmen I didn't know.

"Thank you for bringing my son out here, Mademoiselle Dubois." Cort nodded at the woman as he laid Aimée down. Simone and Henri were immediately at her side. "She is hurt, Rémy. Please go back to Mademoiselle Dubois for a bit."

Rémy obeyed. Blood had spread from Aimée's shoulder, and sweat beaded on her face, but her eyes fluttered open.

"Mère, we'll get you taken care of," Simone said, tears in her eyes.

"Simone, my dear, you don't worry about that. I'm not long for this world. I'll be with my Heavenly Father soon."

"Mère, no!" Cort pulled off his shirt and pressed it to Aimée's wound, hoping to stop the bleeding.

"Please, do not mourn me. I will be in a better place." Aimée took Simone's hand in her left hand and took Cort's with her right. Henri bent his head, and I placed a comforting hand on his shoulder.

"What can we do for you, Mère?" Simone asked.

"Forgive your brother, please. Pray for Antoine and forgive him."

"Mère, his lies and deception and betrayal, he's the reason you got shot." Cort growled.

"I am sure he has his reasons for making the choices that he did." Aimée whispered. "But do not let hate fester in your heart."

"Tante Aimée, you must save your strength." Henri choked the words out.

"Mes chers enfants, remember how much I love you. Always." She closed her eyes as her breathing became even more shallow.

"Mère, no!" Simone buried her face on her mother's shoulder as she sobbed. Henri leaned over and pulled Simone into an embrace. I couldn't stop the tears from falling down my face. Aimée was such a kind, understanding and forgiving woman.

"Mère, please…" Cort, usually so strong and stoic, had tears running down his cheeks. "We need you."

"Listen to Henri," Aimée whispered, then took her last breath.

"Nooo…" Simone wailed. I glanced around, teary-eyed, unable to look at Simone's grief. Everyone in the camp looked stricken, unbelieving of what happened. Aimée was the rock of the Lefevre family and, despite being only a woman, a pillar in the community.

"He is dead to me." Cort growled and stood. "I hold Antoine responsible for his own mother's death. Lewis, Hugo, they are all going to pay."

"Cort, don't do anything rash." Raphael came to his cousin's side. "We have to think things through. Obviously, Aimée thinks Henri will be the one to lead us." Raphael looked at Henri.

"I have no idea what to do!" Henri cried out. "But we should wait longer than three minutes before we forget Aimée and just start making plans."

He stood, almost defensive in his posture. "Besides that, I have absolutely no idea what Aimée meant by saying that. Why am I the one to be in charge? Cort's older than me, and Michael is your father! Why must I come up with the plan?"

"Because my mother told us to listen to you!" Cort exclaimed. "And Jacques was always saying that you were here for a more important reason than just being a trader." Cort took a deep breath to calm himself. Remy crawled onto Simone's lap, tears in his eyes. So much death for this little boy, and the conflict was far from over.

"Well, what if they were wrong? I'm not cut out for this." Henri ran an agitated hand through his hair.

"Henri, just stop and think about it, God put you here..." I tried to help persuade him, give him the confidence he needed, but the look he gave me was frustrated and angry. It scared me a little.

"Leave it alone, Christine. You're not needed here anymore."

CHAPTER FOURTEEN

Henri turned and stalked off toward the lakeshore, leaving me feeling like I had just been punched in the stomach. I shook my head. Henri was angry, but was he also right? Though I didn't do anything to really mess up our plan, could I have done more to make it work? Perhaps I should have been a bit more objective and worked a bit harder. I should have seen Antoine for who he was and exposed him as the traitor. Perhaps I got in Henri's way too much, was I a distraction? Should I have gone home the moment Jacques gave us the return key like Henri had told me to? I turned and trudged in the opposite direction of Henri, needing to get away. Perhaps I would never be beneficial here. Maybe I should just leave. I lowered myself to the ground and leaned against a tree and laid my head on my knees.

"He's just angry and distraught." A low, solid voice came up beside me. I looked up, surprised to see Cort.

"I am so sorry about your mother, Cort," I said with tears in my eyes as he squatted next to me.

"I am sorry she can no longer share her wisdom with us, but I also know that she is in a better place."

"I suppose. I didn't know her long, but she was such a special, irreplaceable woman." I wiped my eyes. "She had a calming effect on everyone she met."

Cort nodded. "I want to tell you that I love Henri like I would love any brother, but he can be quite stubborn. Bullheaded is what Jacques used to call him. Must be a city word."

"Hmm, he is bull-headed, that is for sure." I sighed and stared off in the distance. "But what if Henri is right? Maybe I'm not needed. I can't help but wonder if I have made the situation worse. Perhaps I should just go home."

"You could, but I believe that would be the wrong decision," Cort said. "I have known Henri for three years now, but he has been a different man since you've been here. It is a good thing. Henri will not say it, but he needs you. I believe you should stay here. Your help has been invaluable so far and that will continue to be the case."

"How can you say that, Cort? Since I have been here, your stepfather and now your mother have been murdered. The entire French community is at risk of being massacred."

"This was all happening before you came here, Christine. It's hardly your fault."

"Thank you for saying so, Cort." I couldn't help my surprise at his words. "I must admit, when I first arrived, I had the impression you didn't care for me."

Cort's jaw tightened. "And I must admit, you were right. I was prejudiced against you at the beginning. It takes me a while to trust strangers, especially those from Montreal."

"Yes, your family hinted at that a few times." I replied. "I must confess, I did wonder about why that was."

"Remy's mother is from Montreal. She's still there, as far as I know."

I remained quiet, not wanting to stop Cort from expressing his feelings. I had assumed Remy's mother had died.

"She came here with her parents, her father was a merchant. She was magnificent, a true beauty, and for some reason, she chose me. I thought she loved me. We were married, and she had Remy. I thought we were happy and content, but then one day, she was gone. I never heard from her again. Rumor was she hated living here and needed to move back to Montreal."

"I don't know how any mother could do that, just leave their child," I commented. "And Remy is just the sweetest little boy. It truly is her loss, Cort."

"Thank you. I am so fortunate that I have a sister and mère willing to help raise him." He frowned. "Had a mère."

"Yes," I didn't know what else to say. Words were inadequate for the loss they had just suffered. Cort tightened his jaw again. I wanted to bring up Antoine, but didn't know how Cort would react.

"Henri needs to stop feeling sorry for himself right quick. We need a plan to destroy Lewis. Not only is that lunatic responsible for my mother's death, he somehow coerced my brother into helping him. I just don't understand how he managed to convince Antoine to betray his own family. He is just a boy, a garçon."

I didn't want to point out the fact that Antoine was old enough to make his own decisions, and that he was likely trying to prove that he was more than 'just a boy'.

"If we all think and work together, we will come up with a plan." I stood. "I do thank you for the kind words, Cort. I needed to hear them." He nodded, and we went back to camp.

Aimée had been moved and covered with a wool blanket. I wondered how we would even bury her, with no shovel. I went to Simone and hugged her, hoping to convey my sorrow to her.

"Thank you, Christine," she whispered, clinging to me. "I heard what Henri said to you, and it is not true. We do still need you."

"Thank you for saying so. Cort just told me the same thing."

She smiled. "He may seem unsociable at times, but he does have a kind heart."

"Yes," I said, and was about to tell her that he told me about his wife, but Henri arrived back in the camp, Raphael at his side. It appeared as though Raphael had talked some sense into him.

"Do we have everyone here?" Henri asked, trying to sound confident and in charge.

"Aye." Michael, Raphael's father, nodded.

"All right," Henri said. "We know the best way to stop Lewis, aside from murder, is to get DePeyster to see Lewis's true colors."

"How do you expect to do that?" One of the men I didn't know spoke up.

"Well, Chauvet, we have learned that Lewis plans on assassinating DePeyster and blaming the natives," Henri replied.

"According to him?" A trader with a beard so thick that you couldn't even see his mouth gestured to Logan McIntosh. "Why should we trust him?"

"We can trust him, Bouvier, for a variety of reasons. He's actually been helping us since first being stationed here, after learning how devious Lewis is. Besides, we can verify his

117

information with what we learned from the wonderful covert work of Miss Christine Belanger. She was able to get the same information directly from an inebriated Remington Hugo." He met my eye. "And I would trust both of them with my life." I wondered if that was going to be the only apology I would get from him. I understood he was under a lot of stress at the moment, but his earlier words still hurt.

"I still ain't gonna trust no lobster." Michael Lafontaine crossed his arms over his chest. "Why should I?"

"Because he's your son."

You could have heard a pin drop as everyone looked at Raphael. Even Logan McIntosh looked surprised that Raphael had spoken up.

"What are you blabbering on about, Raphael?" Michael slowly stood.

"He's your son. He came to Michilimackinac in search of you. He was asking around about you and the soldiers pointed him in my direction. I don't see how you can miss it, he looks enough like you."

I gave Michael a closer look and noticed that Raphael was right. Both men were tall, with broad shoulders, and sandy blonde hair, though Logan's was cut neatly and Michael's hung to his shoulders. They had the same brown eyes and other facial features that had an uncanny resemblance.

"My mother was Edith McIntosh." Sergeant McIntosh spoke up, finally confirming what Raphael was saying. "You met her in Edinburgh."

"Edith McIntosh." Recognition dawned on Michael's face. "We were secretly married, but I left her with her parents when I had to come back here for the trading season. Back then, I was just a sailor trying to make contacts so I could become a fur trader. By the time I made it back to Scotland to bring her back to the colonies…well, her father told me she had died."

"That must have been to keep you apart. She didn't die until I was fourteen. My grandfather told her that you'd abandoned her. She never believed him and their relationship was strained from that day on."

"I never did such a thing…" Michael's voice trailed off. 'But I can see her in you as well. I…" He went over to Logan and pulled him into a bear hug. "My deepest apologies, we will talk on

118

this more, but now is not the time. We will have a reunion at a later date, son, but first we need to get rid of Lewis."

"Understood." Logan nodded. Both men turned to Henri, who cleared his throat and continued his speech as if long-lost family members hadn't just reunited.

"Now, I know all of you may have some knowledge or information that we can use. If we're going to stop Lewis, we're going to need everyone," he looked at me and Simone "though I won't force anyone to participate. There's only ten of us and a whole regiment of trained British soldiers, not to mention British traders and merchants that might side with Lewis in a fight."

"There are more French traders and voyageurs who would side with us, if given a choice," Mr. Dubois said. "Young Raphael there recruited who he needed and trusted, but there are more who will join us."

"That is good to know." Henri sighed. "So our next step is pulling together all of the information we know and then discuss our ideas. We have two days before DePeyster is scheduled to return and that's when Lewis is planning his assassination. Let's put our heads together and get to work."

The next day flew by. Marc Chauvet and Armand Bouvier snuck into the village to recruit some more men and learn what they could about the British activities. They learned that Lewis was furious that Henri had escaped. Antoine had moved into the barracks with the British soldiers, while Jacque's house remained empty. Luckily, no other civilians had been injured or taken prisoner as a result of Aimée and Simone's escape. Lewis seemed confident with his new plan to leave Henri alone for the time being. Chauvet and Bouvier were able to get a decent amount of civilians to stand with them against Lewis but, while many of the trappers and traders were upset about the British soldiers and their activities, most just wanted to mind their own business, make their profits and not get involved. Despite all of the business, we were able to have Fr. Gibault come and speak some words over Aimée. We left her wrapped in a thick blanket for the time being, as we knew she would want to be buried next to both of her husbands.

119

We would put her in her final resting place after we defeated Lewis.

We had devised another plan and worked as one unified group to bring it all together. Simone and I had been given muskets and I was quickly reminded of how to use it. I had hunted with my father many times and was a decent shot, but wished I had my own compound bow to use instead of the inaccurate Brown Bess.

"It's almost time." Henri approached me, tossing a bagattaway ball from one hand to the other. We hadn't spoken much since Aimée's death unless it was related to the plan, and he had been cordial, but I missed the close friendship we had formed. "There's still time for you to leave. No one would fault you."

"Really, Henry Beckwith, we're back to that?" I shook my head, irritated. "I'm not leaving and nothing you say will convince me otherwise."

"All right, all right." He tossed me the ball and stuck his hands in his trouser pockets. "Listen, Christine, can we talk?"

"Of course, we're talking right now," I replied, crossing my arms over my chest.

"You're not going to make it easy for me to apologize, are you?" He asked.

"Heavens, whatever would you have to be sorry for?" My response dripped with sarcasm.

"For telling you that we didn't need you anymore. I was wrong about that and I knew I was wrong as I was saying the words. Very wrong, and I am so sorry for hurting you. Can you find it in your heart to forgive me?"

"I already have," I replied. "I actually talked with Père Gibault about it when he was here earlier."

"Yes, he is a good person," Henri replied. "I just worry about you, Christine. Since arriving in the 1770's, I have lost my brother, Jacques, and now Aimée. You know that I've come to care for you. I don't know what I would do if I lost you too. Especially if I had done anything to contribute to your death as I already feel responsible for the death of three people that I cared for dearly."

"Their deaths were hardly your fault, Henri. You can't blame yourself. I just wish you had more faith."

"I have been working on that, but it isn't easy. I know that Aimée's faith until the very end, Simone and Cort's acceptance of her death, and of course, all those years of Jacques's subtle instructions have made me a better person, so I am thankful for that."

"I'm glad." I smiled. "Everything will work out as planned, don't worry. So tell me, when are we going to move out?"

"As discussed, you, Cort and Raphael will be heading over to distract this Olly character. You should be leaving in an hour or so."

"All right." I prayed I could do what needed to be done. As if sensing my doubt, Henri took my hand in his. "We've got this, Christine. We can do this together."

"I am glad to hear you say that, Henri." I squeezed his hand.

CHAPTER FIFTEEN

Logan McIntosh had luckily overheard where Olly was going to be waiting to ambush Major DePeyster, so Cort, Raphael and I made our way to that location. Our job was to find Olly, disarm him and hold him until DePeyster was safely back at the fort. Henri and the rest were going to sneak into the commandant's office so they could grab the papers that showed Lewis was altering the books and selling military goods for his personal profit. Once DePeyster knew of Lewis's schemes, he would have no choice but to court martial the man. Justice would be served for Mark, Aimée and Jacques, as well as all of the people Lewis had oppressed.

"This is the spot," Cort said. "It may be a little while before he gets here."

"Let's find some cover," Raphael suggested. The three of us moved behind a fallen log and laid down on our stomachs, muskets loaded and ready. As I laid down, I felt a lump poke in my stomach. I reached underneath, expecting to find a rock. Instead, I pulled out the bagattaway ball Henri had tossed to me earlier. I had forgotten that I put it in my pocket. I smiled and placed it next to me.

"And now, we wait." I said to myself.

It wasn't ten minutes later when we heard the leaves rustle. Quietly making his way in our direction was a man dressed in deerskin breeches and a lightweight brown shirt. He held a bow and had a quiver thrown over his shoulder. Following him was Antoine. I felt Cort stiffen when he saw his younger brother.

"Just wait," Raphael warned from our hiding place. The two assassins took their own places behind a tree. We knew that timing was imperative for all this to work. DePeyster wasn't due to come through for another half-hour.

Cort nudged Raphael, who silently rolled to his feet, then moved to flank Olly and Antoine.

"There." Antoine pointed and Raphael froze. Luckily, Antoine was gesturing toward the path, not Raphael. On the path was DePeyster's entourage, moving slowly about 100 yards away. Raphael noticed DePeyster as well, and quickly moved to club Olly with his musket. We needed him alive.

"Olly!"

Either Raphael took a wrong step or Antoine had great vision, but at Antoine's warning, Olly turned and shot, his arrow flying into Raphael's shoulder. Cort pushed up from the ground and cocked his gun, but Antoine was ready and pulled his trigger first. Cort fell over, hit in the side. Raphael regained his balance and swung his musket at Antoine, quickly dropping him.

At the sound of the gunshots, the soldiers in DePeyster's guard quickly formed a circle around him, Olly notched an arrow and I pulled the trigger of my musket. My shot missed, but it caused Olly's arrow to fly off into the woods. He pulled out another arrow, then recognized that he didn't have a clear shot any longer. Throwing his bow over his shoulder, he began to run in the direction of the fort.

"He can't get back to Lewis!" Raphael yelled, clutching his shoulder. I didn't have time to reload my firearm, so I reached down and grabbed the bagattaway ball. Harnessing the many years of training I had as a catcher in softball, I aimed and threw. I smiled in satisfaction when I saw it hit him in the head. He fell down hard. Raphael looked at me as if he had never seen anything like that before. I shrugged. It was just like throwing out a girl stealing second.

Major DePeyster and the soldiers guarding him cautiously hastened up the hill.

"What is the meaning of this? Who was shooting? Everyone halt!"

"Major DePeyster! Please." I gestured to Olly and Antoine. "That man over there and the boy, sir, the man with the bow and arrow was sent to kill you." I prayed he would believe me. Our plan involved allowing DePeyster to arrive at Michilimackinac all on his own and startling Lewis into making another move.

"And why would that man wish to harm me?"

I was relieved the major's question was curious and not disbelieving.

"I know this may be difficult to believe, but Leftenant Callum Lewis is trying to take over the fort. He's been targeting the French for some time now, trying to eradicate them. It's almost been like an all-out war since your departure, sir."

Major DePeyster looked troubled. "Quartermaster Askin did mention a concern about the Leftenant, but I brushed it off. Lewis has always been an exemplary soldier." He shook his head. "I'm sorry, but I will require proof." He turned to his entourage. "Take all of the men into custody. We'll sort this out when we get back to the fort."

"Once we get to the fort, sir, we can show you proof of Lewis's treachery." I spoke up.

"Very well, then." The major looked me up and down. "I must say, I don't know that I have ever seen a woman in trousers. Mrs. DePeyster would faint dead away." He began walking back towards his horse as his men helped Olly, Antoine, Cort and Raphael. They were all conscious, though Raphael still had an arrow sticking out of his shoulder and Cort clutched his side where Antoine's bullet had grazed him.

"Yes, sir, I know. Your wife is an inspiration to me when it comes to grace and dignity. I had no choice but to dress like this to stop them from harming you."

"If what you claim turns out to be true, then I will be forever in your debt."

As we prepared to walk toward the fort, I prayed that the rest of our mission would go according to plan. DePeyster would have to believe us once he saw the documents. Perhaps we could even get Antoine or Olly to confess...

"Let's move out, bring them all with us." DePeyster gestured to his men, then me to follow. We arrived at the fort earlier than expected and made our way across the parade grounds. We entered the commandant's house quietly, and it seemed right in the nick of time. Henri stood in the hallway, his hands raised, facing us. Directly in front of him, with his back to us and facing Henri, was Lewis, pointing a pistol at Henri. Upon seeing us enter, Henri seized an opportunity.

"You're going to kill me anyway, Lewis, make me an example or whatnot, but can you at least tell me why? Why the French? What do you hope to accomplish by eradicating them from the straits area?"

"Once you and DePeyster are out of my way, I'll be able to get rid of all the French. DePeyster and his predecessors should never have allowed them to remain in Michilimackinac. They should have been eradicated long ago. Anyone loyal to Britain would agree."

"And what about these documents?" Henri held up the papers we knew would implicate Lewis. "Would any man loyal to Britain feel it is within his right to sell weapons and ammunition to the Indians and then lie on the inventory papers?"

"I'll need money to reinforce this fort, make it more formidable and more profitable than ever before. Besides, as far as anyone of import is concerned, it was DePeyster who was stealing from the crown."

My heart flooded with relief and I sent up a quick prayer of thanks. This was going better than I could have imagined.

"And what of Jacques?" Henri asked. "Did you plan his death, did you have him killed?"

Lewis gave a maniacal laugh. "Jacques's own so-called son did the deed to prove his loyalty to me. Jacques Evans never even realized it was the boy that shot him. I must admit, that was quite brilliant on my part. Let the boy prove his allegiance to me and get rid of one of the leading French traders in the fort. The old man had far too much influence in the French community. That part of my plan worked out quite well for me, to be sure. The stupid boy doesn't realize I am simply using him. Naturally, I will discard of him as soon as his usefulness wears out."

I glanced at Antoine, whose face showed a look of hurt, pain, and anger all in one. I couldn't imagine what was going through his mind, knowing that he had only been a pawn in Lewis's plan. Knowing that he had betrayed his own family and even caused the deaths of his mother and stepfather with his misplaced loyalty.

I looked back at Henri, who gritted his teeth. I shook my head at him. As angry as he was, he couldn't attack Lewis, not when we were so close to attaining justice, and especially not with DePeyster watching.

"You deserve to rot in prison." Henri finally said.

"Yet, it is you who will rot in your grave first." Lewis cocked his flintlock pistol.

"I have heard quite enough, Leftenant Lewis." DePeyster commanded at the same time Rebecca DePeyster entered the hallway, right next to us.

"Arnet, thank goodness you're back!" She cried.

Lewis looked back at us, shocked, then turned and pointed his pistol right at me. Everything happened in slow motion next. As Lewis pulled the trigger, Antoine, still tied up, threw himself in front of me. The bullet hit his chest.

With a yell, Henri grabbed his hunting knife from the hilt of his belt and grabbed Lewis, then placed the knife to his throat.

I froze, wanting to help Antoine, but one glance at the boy confirmed that he wasn't breathing, so I had to stop Henri from making the mistake of killing Lewis in cold blood.

"Henri, don't! We have him," I begged. "We will get justice."

Henri paused as if thinking. "I know," he replied. "This prisoner is for you, Major." He shoved Lewis towards the door while keeping a tight hold on him.

DePeyster, who had managed to embrace his distraught wife, nodded.

"Thank you, young man. The entire Mackinac Straits area is in your debt."

"Sir, look out!" Cort yelled and threw himself at Remington Hugo. With all of the distractions, no one had seen Hugo creep into the hallway until he had his pistol trained on Major DePeyster's head. As Cort's body hit the Sergeant, the pistol fell to the ground. Cort laid Hugo unconscious with an awkward, hands-tied-together punch, but in the scuffle, Lewis threw his head back at Henri, hitting him hard in the nose. Henri fell backwards, his knife clattering to the floor. Lewis grabbed Hugo's pistol from the ground and pointed it at Henri again.

"Goodbye, Beckwith," he growled, cocking the firearm. "Good riddance."

"No!" I quickly grabbed Hugo's pistol from the ground, aimed, and pulled the trigger. Lewis cried out in pain and fell, wounded in the arm.

127

"Get these men taken care of at once." DePeyster ordered as I rushed to Henri, who was now sitting up. I threw my arms around him and he gave me a tight hug.

"We did it." He laughed, despite the blood dripping from his nose. "I can't believe it."

"We did! And Lewis confessed to everything, right in front of DePeyster." I shook my head.

"Apparently, Lewis doesn't know that when the villain gives his evil monologue at the end of the movie, it always backfires." Henri and I both stood. DePeyster's men were already leading Lewis, Hugo and Olly to the guardhouse, while Raphael and Cort knelt next to Antoine.

"Is he..." I couldn't even finish the question, for I already knew the answer.

"He's dead." Raphael replied. "Probably the second the bullet hit him."

"He saved my life." I whispered. "But why would Lewis shoot me when he could have shot you, Henri?"

"To hurt me," Henri explained. "He told me before you all came in that he enjoyed the look of defeat on me more, like when he held Aimée and Simone. Killing me wouldn't bring him as much satisfaction as killing those I love and watching me suffer for it."

"The man is truly cruel." I shuddered.

"And I feel duped by him." Major DePeyster spoke up. "John Askin made a few comments about not feeling right where he was concerned."

"Many were fooled by Lewis and his men, sir." Henri looked down at Antoine.

"Sir, I know Raphael here isn't part of the British army, but could we have the post doctor take a look at him?" Cort asked.

I had forgotten about Raphael's shoulder wound. The arrow had yet to be removed. He had a pained look on his face that he tried to conceal when I glanced at him.

"Yes, yes, but of course." DePeyster nodded. "I have you all to thank for stopping that demonic man. As a matter of fact, all three of you look like you need to see the post doctor. Go on, all of you, you are dismissed." Cort escorted Raphael out the door.

"Thank you all from the both of us," Mrs. DePeyster added. "I must say, I am sorry for ostracizing you, Miss Belanger, and I will

128

add that it is rather shocking to see you in men's breaches. I also realize now that you were loyal to your fiancé."

"Yes, ma'am." I blushed as Henri pulled me closer to him. Out of the corner of my eye, I saw two British soldiers pick up Antoine's body and move him out of the house.

"We should get Père Gibault to perform your nuptials right now," Mrs. DePeyster continued.

"With all due respect, Mrs. DePeyster, my future bride has made it quite clear that she would like to be married in Montreal. I have finally been convinced to grant her that wish." Henri's words relieved me. He always had an explanation.

"But…"

"In fact, she has a cousin who is a priest and she would like him to perform the ceremony."

"I do appreciate the offer, Mrs. DePeyster, but Henri is right." I replied.

"And now, with Jacques and Aimée dead, I was thinking that we might just stay in Montreal." Henri added. It will be nice to return to our families."

I wondered if the DePeysters could tell how emotional and happy Henri was.

"Very well." DePeyster leaned down and gave his wife a quick kiss on the cheek. "I'm sorry to leave you again so soon, my love, but I must make sure that all the guilty parties are charged and confined properly and that all the innocent men must be released. It may take a while for me to sort this all out."

"Of course," Rebecca answered.

Henri pulled my arm and led me out the door. I felt a wave of my own emotions flare up when I saw the blood stain where Antoine had died. A tear fell down my cheek. It was a bittersweet day. Lewis, Hugo and all the corrupt British soldiers would be court martialed and punished. Attempted mutiny was dealt with harshly, but had it all been worth it? So much life had been lost, so many lives destroyed. Mark Beckwith, Jacques, Aimée, Antoine…how many others? I realized I didn't know how Henri's mission had gone prior to our arrival and I wasn't sure I knew how to broach the question. Luckily, I didn't have to.

"Other than Antoine, there was only one other casualty," Henri spoke softly, as if reading my thoughts. "Everything was going perfect, but then a British trader blew our cover and... Michael Lafontaine was killed."

"No! That cannot be!"

"He died a hero, Christine. If Michael hadn't taken the focus off Sergeant McIntosh, it would have been Logan who was killed."

"So he saved his own son in the end." I choked on the words.

"He did. I expect Logan has already told Raphael." Henri and I were almost back to the Evans's home.

"It's so sad that Michael died, just as he found his older son and just as he was connecting with his younger son. I feel so sorry for Logan and Raphael." I sighed and wiped a tear from my eye. "So, I suppose that's it. Play the theme song, roll the end credits. It's time to go home."

"Yes, finally." Henri smiled. "What's the first thing you want to do when you get home?"

"Go across the bridge that will now be there and get a burger from Clyde's," I replied, referring to the quaint drive-in burger joint in St. Ignace. "And use a toilet that flushes." I smiled. "What about you?"

"Clyde's onion rings do sound good, but not before I take a nice, long, hot shower," he replied. "Then, I will take my girl across the bridge, get some food, and eat while we watch the sunset off the lake at the Straits State Park."

"That sounds just perfect."

We walked into Jacques's house.

"There will be some very tough goodbyes," Henri said.

"True." I agreed thinking specifically of the bond I had formed with Simone. Then there was Raphael, Cort, and little Remy. When we left, it would be for good. There would be no keeping up with each other via social media.

"You would think this would be an easy choice," Henri said. "But there are many things about this time period that I will miss."

"I know what you mean." I was about to add another comment when Raphael, Cort, Simone and Logan McIntosh came in. I dashed to Raphael and hugged him.

"I am so glad you're all here safe!" I turned and hugged Simone, then Cort and, just because I was so happy, I hugged Sergeant McIntosh. Simone's eyes were red and Raphael was stone-faced.

"I cannot believe Antoine is gone now too." Simone cried.

130

"I know he made some poor decisions in his short life, but remember, he made the right choice in the end." Cort put a comforting arm around his sister.

"Raphael, Sergeant McIntosh, I am so sorry about your father." I hugged Raphael again.

"He tried to be a good father, especially at the end." Raphael shrugged, trying to act as if it didn't bother him, though I knew it did.

"I do wish I'd have gotten to know him better," McIntosh said, "but I believe we came to terms in the short time he knew me."

"So, now what?" Raphael asked, focusing on me. "Are you going to get Gibault and have your ceremony and take over this house and all of Jacques's holdings and have your own family?"

"Not exactly," Henri answered. "We're actually going home. We'll continue our relationship there."

"What of Jacques's business?" Cort asked.

"You have much more of a right to run it than I ever did," Henri replied. "And you have a son who can learn from you and one day take it over."

Cort smiled. "That means much to me, Henri. I am honored." He reached out and clasped Henri's hand.

"I will certainly miss you Cort, and little Remy." Henri looked around. "Where is the little guy?"

"Mrs. DuBois will be bringing him here after her husband picks her up from the camp. We had to make sure it was safe enough for him to return."

"Of course." I nodded.

"How long until you both leave?" Simone asked.

"Within the week," Henri answered. "We'll make sure everything is settled here, then Christine and I will go home."

"I'm going with you."

CHAPTER SIXTEEN

Henri and I both turned to look at Raphael.

"What do you mean?" Henri asked, concern etched on his face.

"I don't need your permission." Raphael replied. I was surprised to see him looking so sullen.

"That's true, of course, but..." I began to say.

"Could I speak with you out back, Christine?" Raphael interrupted me. "Just you?"

I glanced at Henri, who shrugged, then nodded at Raphael as I followed him out back.

"Raphael, what..."

Once again, Raphael interrupted me, this time by attempting to kiss me. I quickly shoved him away.

"Raphael Lafontaine, what is wrong with you? What was that for?"

"I'm in love with you, Christine. Surely you know that by now."

I wanted to remind him that we were just teenagers, but I realized that people matured differently in the 1770's. Raphael had been on his own and working with the voyageurs for close to four years already.

"I most certainly did not know. How was I to realize that? You are a flirt, Raphael, you act toward me the same way you act toward every other woman."

"But what I feel with you is different. You continually surprise me. I enjoy talking with you, learning more about you on a daily basis. You are unlike any other woman I have known."

Because I don't belong here. "That's because we're friends, Raphael. I like you yes, but only as a friend. Nothing more."

"So you're going to go through with this marriage to Henri once you get back to Montreal."

"Perhaps not right away as we once thought, but I do care for him."

Raphael sighed. "That isn't what I wanted to hear, but I still plan on going to Montreal with you."

"Why?" I asked. "This is your home."

"I have lost my father. Even though he wasn't always there for me, he did teach me everything he knew. I have also lost the people who were most like parents to me, Jacques and Aimée. Cort will do very well with the business, Henri is right about that. Logan is in the British army and may be transferred elsewhere, especially with the rebellion in the colonies. I wouldn't be surprised if Simone gives her heart to him soon. I just don't have any reason to stay here. I need a place to start new. Perhaps that place can be Montreal."

"Maybe," I sighed. Raphael brought up some good points, and I believed he wanted to get away from all the bad memories.

"I think we should discuss this with Henri. It's his future as well." I wasn't sure what to tell Raphael next. Clearly, he would know something was up when Henri and I didn't really go to Montreal.

"All right," Raphael said, resigned. "We'll talk more tomorrow. I should report to my crew leader and tell him that I'm leaving either way."

"If that's what you feel is necessary," I replied, then went back into Jacques house.

The next couple of days flew by as we prepared to leave. I was able to say a farewell to the DePeysters and even heard Major DePeyster recite the poem he wrote for Mrs. DePeyster after her pet squirrel, Timmy, died.

Logan McIntosh had been promoted to Lieutenant by DePeyster and he formally started courting Simone. She seemed very happy and content with McIntosh, in spite of his occupation. Cort stepped right into Jacques business as he already had very good relationships with the trading partners. Most comforting was that Lewis, Hugo, Olly and several other soldiers who had been loyal to Lewis were being escorted back East and then on to England to await court martial. Justice would be served.

I felt good about leaving with DePeyster in command. It seemed as though everyone was going to have a successful future. Henri had decided to tell Raphael everything, including the truth about where we were really going. He took the information surprisingly well, though I feel he didn't quite believe it.

"I'd still like to go with you," he said, crossing his arms over his chest.

"Raphael, you realize that it is a whole new world, right?" Henri asked. "You're only sixteen. They would place you with a foster family since you have no other family and you will no longer be able to do whatever you want. You would have to go to school."

"I will adapt," Raphael replied stubbornly. "How hard can it be?"

"Life is very different from where we came from. I wouldn't even know where to start explaining it all to you." Henri insisted. "It's not that I don't want you to come, you're my best friend and I'm quite sure that my parents would take you in and raise you as their own, but like I said, it is such a different world."

"You know, Henri," I spoke up. "We have our story established for telling our parents what happened to us. We could tell them that Raphael was there long before we were and that his parents died while imprisoned. He would never have known the outside world, which would be a believable reason for him not knowing certain things."

"That is true," Henri replied.

We had come up with a decent storyline as to where we had been. We would tell our parents and the police that we were kidnapped and had been held prisoner on a nearby uninhabited island by a deranged man named Lewis, appropriately. We had finally escaped the lunatic's clutches, but Jack Evans and Mark Beckwith had died heroes while trying to save us. Our abductor had been killed in the struggle as well. We had been able to make our way back to the mainland on a makeshift raft, but we couldn't remember exactly which island or where the shack we had been held in was located. If there were any gaps in our story, we would just pretend we were too traumatized to remember the details.

"Are you sure you want to do this?" Henri asked Raphael. "I'm not sure there will ever be a way back. The key may not work again."

"I'm sure. The 21st Century sounds like a good time for a new start."

"Well, all right, then." Henri smiled. "We were planning on leaving early tomorrow morning. Will you be ready?"

"I could be ready right now." Raphael answered.

"No, tomorrow morning, early." As sneaky as it might be, we will leave a note and depart before daybreak. It will be awkward to explain why we are going to Montreal, but leaving by way of a tunnel under the cannon.

"I cannot believe you're going to leave already," Simone said as we walked along the water that evening. "You have only been here for a month, yet you have become my dearest friend." Since she already knew we were from a different time, Henri and I agreed to tell Simone the true plan. She would be able to smooth over any questions the others might have.

"And you, mine." I hated goodbyes. "I will never forget you, Simone. Never ever." I hugged her. "I only wish you could come with us."

"I don't think I could handle living in your future world." She smiled. "Besides, I would hate to leave Cort and Remy and Leftenant McIntosh, of course."

"I know," I groaned, then pulled out my phone. "This may sound strange, but will you take a picture with me? So I can always remember you."

"Take a what?" Simone was understandably confused.

"It's like a painting, kind of." I explained, looking at the phone screen. I still had 11 % battery left. "Using this futuristic device."

"I suppose, if you say it's safe." Simone still looked wary.

"Absolutely," I said. Getting close to her, I held the phone out. "Look at that screen and smile."

"Goodness, is that…what...is that me?"

"Yes, ma'am, it is." I smiled. "I will be capturing this moment for eternity."

"What a wonderful idea." Simone smiled and I snapped the selfie.

"There." I showed her the picture. "Now there is no way I will ever forget you."

"If I didn't know any better, I'd think this was witchcraft." She shook her head.

"Nope, just a thing called technology." I assured her.

"I will never forget you, Christine Belanger, even if I don't have a futuristic painting of you." She pulled me into an embrace. "Take care of yourself, and please watch out for Henri and Raphael. Especially Raphael. He has changed much since the day his father died."

"I will." I promised her. She was definitely right about Raphael. He had been melancholy since our conversation about our feelings toward one another. "As much as I hate to say it, we should head back to Jacques's."

"Yes, I suppose," Simone replied, and we ended our last walk together.

CHAPTER SEVENTEEN

"I feel like a thief, just sneaking out like this," Raphael said as we made our way to the cannon at the water's edge. There was a part of me that worried the key wouldn't work. If it didn't, what would we do? Where would we go? Henri put an arm around me comfortingly.

"It will be alright," he whispered.

"I know."

We finally reached the cannon, and Henri knelt down and moved the dirt away from the trap door. He then took out the key. "Well, here goes nothing." He slid the key in the lock and turned it. As it clicked, I released a breath. The hatch opened.

"Let's go." Henri said.

We dropped through the opening and down into the tunnel.

"Well, I must admit, I really wasn't sure I believed you, but...well, I must say I'm really starting to." Raphael shook his head in amazement. I took my phone out so I could light the way.

"You should know by now that I don't lie," Henri replied. We made our way through the tunnel, then reached the ladder that lead up to the priest's cellar and climbed out.

"When was this put up?" Raphael came up behind me, pushing at the barrier that kept visitors from falling down into the cellar.

"We did it!" Henri whooped when he saw the modern setting of the priest's house. "Christine, we're home!"

I turned and he swept me up in his arms and spun me around.

"Let's get to our families."

We quickly made our way out of the fort and toward the visitor center, where I knew we would be able to exit the fort without triggering any alarms.

"What in the world…" Raphael stopped, eyes wide at the sight of the bridge and the cars crossing. "How…what is that monstrosity?"

"That, my friend, is the Mackinac Bridge." Henri clapped Raphael on the back. "We warned you that this was a different world."

"You weren't lying!"

We continued walking, heading toward the center of Mackinaw City. As planned, I would go to my parents house to let them know I was home and Raphael and Henri would go to the police station to make the report, since his family was on the island. I pulled out my phone. 6:19 AM, and 8% battery life. My parents would likely be awake by now, getting ready for the day. I had to stop myself from running as fast as I could.

"I'll see you both soon!" I said when we parted ways.

My heart pounded in excitement as I approached the comfortable home that I had grown up in. I would never take it for granted again. I opened the door with the hide-a-key, then stepped into the mud room.

"Who's there?" I heard my mother's voice, tired and sad.

"It's me, Mom." I entered the kitchen. Both of my parents stood, and it wasn't even a second later that I was being pulled into the biggest hug I think I had ever had.

"My baby, my baby girl is back." My mother had tears running down her face, and my father's eyes were shimmering as well.

"It's been quite the experience, Mom, but I'm home. By the grace of God, I am home for good."

That day passed quickly. Everyone accepted our story as fact, and the authorities said they would go and search some nearby abandoned islands, which, of course, would be to no avail. With my parents, I had visited everyone in my family. They didn't want to leave my side, and I couldn't blame them. My mother had insisted on bringing me to the center of the city so that I could meet up with Henri, Raphael and the Beckwiths so we could all have dinner together.

Mr. and Mrs. Beckwith were very kind and thanked me over and over again for helping to bring their son home. They talked excitedly with my parents as we waited for a table at the Keyhole Bar and Grill, one of my favorite restaurants. I had texted Sadie and she was going to meet us there as well.

"Of course, Mom and Dad cried when I told them about Mark," Henri said. "After we disappeared, they couldn't live on the island anymore, because of the memories. They bought a house in Indian River, right on Burt Lake."

"That is a nice area, and Indian River isn't so far away." I commented. "A half-hour or so. It's less time to get there than to take a ferry to get to the Island."

"That is true," Henri nodded. "They never expected to see either me or Mark again. They've already decided to take in Raphael, with absolutely no hesitation. My dad's going to check with your brother, the one who is a lawyer, tomorrow about paperwork for adoption."

"That's wonderful." I looked at Raphael to see what he thought of the arrangement, but he simply stared at the cars and the people around us. He jumped high when the Star Line ferry blew its horn.

"Sacrebleu! What in the world…"

"It's the boat over there." Henri pointed. "No worries, you'll get used to all of this."

"C'est manifique." Raphael shook his head.

"We'll both be attending Inland Lakes High School come fall." Henri continued with his update. "Also, I know the Keyhole isn't quite Clyde's, but it still has wonderful food." Henri smiled and took my hand. "We'll go over the bridge tomorrow, I promise. Burgers and a sunset."

"I can't wait, and I'm really glad that we all got a long, hot shower." I smiled back. Henri hadn't had his hair cut yet, but had been able to shave. It was strange, seeing his smooth cheeks instead of the rugged beard. It made him look younger. It was also strange to see both Henri and Raphael in jeans and the button-up shirts that they had obtained from a quick trip to the Cheboygan Walmart.

141

"That shower, as you call it, is quite amazing." Raphael said. "And Henri's father asked if we wanted to play football on the school team this fall. He's going to show me how the game is played on that...thing that talks and..." He shook his head in amazement.

"The television." I smiled. Raphael had a lot to learn.

"Christine!" A familiar voice squealed and I was almost tackled by the blonde whirlwind known as my best friend. "I was so, so, so happy when your sister sent the group text to the team saying you were all right, then you texted me...what on earth happened?"

"I'm not sure you would believe me if I told you." I smiled, knowing that someday soon, I would tell Sadie the whole truth. She was the one person who just might believe the story. "Sadie, may I introduce you to Henry Beckwith," Henry took my hand in his, "and Raphael Lafontaine."

"Of course I remember who Henry Beckwith is, Christine." Sadie smiled. "And the news is all over the city about what happened to you all, what a perfectly dreadful experience! I am just so glad you're all back home and safe, well, with the exception of Mark Beckwith and Old Man Evans. I am so sorry for your loss." Sadie turned to Raphael. "And I am glad to welcome you to Mackinaw City, Raphael."

"Thank you. It has been an interesting experience to say the least." Raphael smiled his most charming smile at my friend.

"We'll make sure you get acclimated to the city." Sadie answered him.

"I'll look forward to it," Raphael said. "Now, Henri and Christine keep talking about this food item called a cheeseburger. Have you ever had one yourself?"

"Oh dear, Raphael, you surely have a lot to learn." Sadie grabbed Raphael's arm and pulled him into the Keyhole as they called our name.

Henry and I laughed. Sadie had no idea. As the two went in, followed by our parents, I pulled back on Henry's arm. He gave me a quick kiss.

"It is so hard to believe how this all worked out," I said. "I mean, like with your parents moving to Indian River, we won't need to take the ferry to see each other."

"Yes, however, there are still many unanswered questions. And I would like to somehow find out what happened to Cort, Remy, Simone and Logan."

"Lewis and Hugo as well," I replied. "I'm sure I can get us into the records room at the fort. We can find out..."

"Christine!"

I turned at the familiar voice of Dylan Rodriguez, looking good in his baseball pants, a dry-fit baseball shirt, and dark blonde hair poking from his backwards baseball cap. Henry stepped closer to me and took my hand in his.

"I heard what happened." Dylan took a step forward. "I must say, I am glad you're back and okay. I was hoping to take you to dinner."

I glanced at Henry. Just a month ago, I would have given so much to hear words like that from Dylan, I would have been so eager for his approval. But so much had happened and I realized in that moment, even if I wasn't dating Henry, that I didn't need the approval of any boy, or really, anyone. I stepped away from Henry.

"Now that it's closer to basketball season?" I felt triumphant when I saw Dylan's face redden. "Dylan, it's kind of you to say that you're glad I'm back. But there is something I should have said to you some time ago." I took a deep breath, gathering my courage. "You can be a very nice guy when you want to be, but you can also be a real jerk when you're around certain friends." I then turned and went into the Keyhole, proud that I had finally stood up for myself.

That night, my parents held a 'welcome home' bonfire. My siblings, nieces and nephews were all there, as well as some close friends and the Beckwiths.

"Finally, something familiar to me." Raphael smiled, staring at the flames. "Although I'm not quite sure about this...this thing Sadie just brought to me. Before I even had one, she asked if I wanted more." He held up a s'more.

143

"Go ahead and eat it," I laughed, "you will not regret it." I patted his back and moved to my sister, Rachel. She hugged me tightly.

"Ohh, Christine, you don't know how relieved we are to have you back. We thought we had lost you forever."

"Glad your favorite player is back, you mean." I was only half-teasing.

"Christine, you could quit the team tomorrow and never play another sport again and I wouldn't care. Don't get me wrong, you are invaluable to the team, but you are absolutely priceless and irreplaceable as a sister." She looked at me. "I realize how difficult it must be as the youngest child in this family. Sometimes, I feel as though I underachieved in my life, based on the careers that Becca and Anna and Sean have had and that Andrew will undoubtedly have."

"I never realized that," I replied. Rachel always seemed so confident with the choices she made in life.

"Yes, so trust me when I tell you, you'll find your path, Christine."

"Thank you, Rachel. You are the best sister-teacher-coach a girl could ask for."

"Mmmhmm." Rachel smiled and nodded toward Henry, who was tossing a football with my seven-year-old nephew, Daniel. "And by the way, I like him. We all approve."

"Yes, I like him too," I replied, hoping she couldn't see my blushing face.

I was able to visit with all of my family members as well as the Beckwiths. As I returned to the bonfire, my six-year-old niece, Teresa jumped into my lap, giving me the biggest hug and kiss. I looked at her and sent up a prayer of thanks, not just for my family, but also for the adventure I had just returned from, an adventure which had given me confidence and an appreciation for all that I had once taken for granted.

EPILOGUE

One Week Later

"Henry!" I smiled as I exited the fort's guide shack and hugged him. It had been a great week. I had been able to jump right back into my work schedule and athletic practices. I was thankful that my co-workers had been so distracted by my disappearance and reappearance that they had completely forgotten about the key that had sent me on that adventure in the first place. It was hard to believe that if Samuel had not found the key, I never would have had my experience. "What are you doing here?" I asked Henry.

"I had to come and see my girl." He smiled. "Can you join me for a walk?"

"Of course." We headed for Michilimackinac State Park, the grounds that bordered the fort next to the lake. The park had a wonderful view of the bridge and the island.

"How are your football workouts going?" I asked.

"They're going well. Raphael is picking the game up very easily. Coach is looking at having him be a running back. He's quick."

"And what position does he have you playing?"

"Tight end and outside linebacker. Apparently he is impressed by the way I tackle."

"Well, I remember when you tackled Hugo that time he was beating up Raphael. I was impressed by the way you took him down."

"Well, thank you. I'm actually looking forward to the season, and, strangely enough, school."

"I'm looking forward to your season too. I love watching football. We don't have a school team here in Mac City, so with you playing, I'll have a good reason to watch all of your games."

"I'm glad you'll be there." Henry smiled. "Speaking of Hugo, I was finally able to do some research. The internet has gotten so much better since I used it last."

"Yes," I agreed. "What did you find out?"

"Not a lot of details, but I did find some records. It seems as though Cort and Remy lived long lives, as I found their burial records. We can even go and visit their graves." He shook his head. "It is so odd to say that. Simone and Logan McIntosh were married and had five children, can you believe that?"

"Marvelous! I wonder if they have any descendants still in the area."

"That would be cool to find out, even though it would be strange to meet them."

"What about Hugo and Lewis?" I asked.

"I found that information too, and it really troubles me." Henry gestured to the gazebo that stood in the park near the Mackinac Point Lighthouse.

"Sounds ominous," I replied.

"The ship they were put on to face a court martial in England was apparently sunk by an American privateer. Hugo was shot dead. Lewis was listed as being 'lost at sea'."

"Lost at sea." My heart skipped a beat. "So we don't know if he died for sure or if he somehow escaped." I shook my head. "So that madman could have survived."

"We can't really know for sure, Christine," Henry confirmed. "It's still good to know that our world wasn't destroyed because of him. He is surely dead by now."

"That's true enough. But does he have descendants?" I sighed. "Well, we cannot dwell on that now, I suppose. It is wonderful to hear about Cort, Remy and Simone, though." I pulled out my phone and flipped to the picture I had taken with Simone. "She was such a good friend."

"Yes, but we have good friends here, too." Henry said. "And a very promising future ahead."

"Yes, a future I look forward to experiencing."

146

Timmy

See, where the giddy circling Tim
lies motionless at last.
What though no squirrel ran like him
grim death could run as fast.
Cease then, my fair, o cease to mourn
for guiltless Timmy's sake,
since there's no living creature born
but death will overtake.
-A. S. DePeyster

Read on for an excerpt from the next book in the Key to Mackinac adventure...

BEYOND THE ISLAND

I looked around and saw Rafe stomping away toward the parking lot.

"If anyone can knock some sense into that boy, it's you, Sadie." Christine told me. I nodded and went in the direction that Rafe took. I hoped Christine was right.

It didn't take me long to realize that Rafe wasn't meeting anyone from the bonfire or going to Henry's truck. It was lucky I was used to walking just about everywhere as Rafe seemed to be heading all the way into town. Or...was he?

I kept following him and I frowned as he neared the Colonial fort. Rafe quickly scaled the chain-link fence that surrounded the fort and it's outbuildings. I hurried to keep up and climbed over the fence myself. What in the world was Rafe doing?

I finally caught up with him at the guide shack, where Christine, Henry, and their co-workers kept their historical outfits and other supplies.

"Rafe?"

He jumped in surprise, and I was taken aback at what he was doing. He was wearing what had to be Henry's work pants and he had just pulled on a colonial shirt over his ribbed tee.

"Sadie, what are you doing here?" He exclaimed.

"I wanted to talk with you about what just happened, but instead, I should be asking you the same question." I retorted.

"Whatever." Rafe shrugged.

"How did you even get in here?" I asked. "And what do you think you're doing?"

"Henry locks up sometimes, so he had a key. I'm just borrowing it."

I glanced at the table and saw two keys, a modern-looking house key and an old skeleton key. "Oh no, no, no, Rafe, is this what I think it is?" I ran my finger along the cool metal. It had to be the key that took both Henry and Christine back to the 1770's. "Rafe, what are you going to do? Are you planning on going back? Without even telling anyone?"

He ran a hand through his hair. "Just for a visit. That's all. I want to see my brother and some other friends. I…I have to, Sadie."

The vulnerable look on his face touched something in me. I'm not sure why I responded the way I did, but I replied. "All right. But I'm coming with you."

He looked shocked. "Why? No way. Sadie, that's crazy."

"Either you let me come with you or I call Henry right now." I held up my phone. I wasn't sure why I was asserting myself like this, but something made me want to have an adventure like Christine had.

Rafe took a deep breath. "You're serious." He was clearly annoyed.

"I am dead serious," I moved towards the closet that I knew held Christine's clothing for work.

"Well then, hurry up," Rafe said. I quickly pulled on a skirt and short gown over my t-shirt and leggings, grateful that the clothes were one-size fits most and Christine had the same shoe size I did.

"All right, lead on." I looked at Rafe, finally seeing him in his natural apparel. He looked different, but much more comfortable than in his usual jeans and button-up checkered shirt. He nodded and I followed him around the palisade to the watergate, then into the priest's house, right next to Ste. Anne's Church. I quickly sent a text to Christine, letting her know what we were doing and asking her to cover for us with our parents. Before she could reply, I put my phone on airplane mode and we hopped the barrier. We went down into the cellar of the basement. We quickly found the trapdoor and climbed down into the tunnel. When we were in the tunnel, Rafe pulled out the skeleton key and unlocked the door.

"Where did you even get the key? I thought Christine had hidden it somewhere safe. A place that not even I knew about." Which kind of rubbed me the wrong way, as I was her best friend, but I had to respect her need for secrecy.

Rafe pulled out a mini flashlight as we made our way down the dirt path. "I learned where she kept it when I first got to this time period. It was in some hidden crevice in their back shed. As you probably know, Henry and I hung out at the Belanger house when we got back from Clyde's before going to the beach, so I slipped out there and took it. Like I said, I had to. I'm..." He couldn't even say the words.

"Homesick?" I asked. "It's okay to talk about your feelings, Rafe."

"Not where I grew up," he replied, then fell silent.

I wasn't very good with directions or estimating distance, but it felt as if we were walking quite a bit more than just to the cannon platform, which is where Christine had come out and arrived in 1775.

"Did it take this long last time?" I asked.

"I don't recall. I was still taking in the fact that time travel was possible." Rafe quipped.

"So do you have any idea where the key even came from? As you said, the whole idea of time travel is just crazy. If I didn't know what I know and...met you and everything. I wouldn't believe it myself."

"You talk too much, has anyone ever told you that?" Rafe grumbled.

"Sure they have, I am an inquisitive person, so I have a lot of questions. I also think out loud a lot, so excuse me for trying to reason through things."

"It's just that no one here can stand silence. They always need music or the TV on, or even nature noises from a machine while trying to sleep." He shook his head. "Rediculous."

"Well, that's true, I am guilty of always needing my music on."

"What you listen to can hardly be called music."

I bristled. "Just because you don't like country, doesn't mean..." I shook my head. It wasn't worth it. He was always slamming my taste in music and his mind would never be changed. "You didn't answer my question about the key."

151

"How would I know, Sadie? Like you, I wouldn't have believed any of this if I hadn't personally experienced it."

Finally, the tunnel sloped upwards and there was a ladder in front of us.

"Here we go." Rafe pulled himself up the rungs, flashlight in his mouth. When he reached the top he clicked the light off, then pushed open a trapdoor. I followed him and stepped onto solid ground, but ran into his back when he stopped suddenly.

"What are you doing?" I gave him a small shove in the shoulder.

"No. This isn't right." Rafe was dumbfounded. I quickly moved around him to see what had shocked him so much. My stomach dropped just a bit when I saw what he was looking at.

"Uhhh...Rafe?"

He rubbed his jaw. "Fort Mackinac. We're on the island." He glanced at the flagpole, which had a British flag flying from it.

"Rafe, I don't know as much history as Christine, but I don't think we've gone back to 1775."

Author's Note

I hope you enjoyed reading my newest novel! It was extremely fun for me to write and research this book because of my love for Northern Michigan. I have had a love of Mackinaw City, Mackinac Island, and the Straits of Mackinaw for as long as I can remember. Some of my very best memories come from that area. I have taken countless family vacations there growing up, and was able to work for Mackinac State Historic Parks for a few summers. Even now, I feel the need to visit the area at least once a year. It was, in fact, my years working at Colonial Michilimackinac that inspired this novel. There were many times when my Historic Interpreter co-workers and I wondered what it would be like to go back in time and meet the characters that lived at Michilimackinac. Some of the actual historic figures associated with the fort in 1775 include Major Arent Schuyler and Rebecca DePeyster (and Timmy the Squirrel!), John and Archange Askin, and Father Pierre Gibault. The setting of the fort is historically accurate as well. However, the Lefevre family, Lafontaine family, Belanger family, Beckwith family, as well as Hugo Remington, Callum Lewis and Logan McIntosh are all fictitious. As far as I can tell, there never was a plot to overthrow Major DePeyster in 1775.

Many of the places mentioned, such as the Michilimackinac State Park, Colonial Michilimackinac, the Keyhole Bar and Grill, and Clyde's Drive-In are real and can be visited today! Make sure you stop by these awesome places if you are ever in the Straits area.

Images

Arent Schuyler
DePeyster

Rebecca DePeyster

Fr.
Pierre Gibault

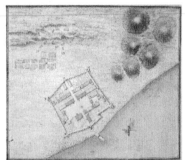

A Colonial Sketch of Fort
Michilimackinac

The Water Gate

Ste. Anne's Church-Interior

The Commandant's House and the Soldier's Barraks

The Cellar of the Priest's House

The Black Hole

The Guardhouse

Colonial Michilimacinac Today

About the Author

Erica Marie LaPres Emelander is a middle school social studies/religion teacher and lives in Grand Rapids, MI. Erica has always enjoyed reading and writing, and with her love of history and God, she has incorporated all four loves into her writing. When not working on and researching her books, Erica can be found coaching middle and high school sports, being a youth minister, and spending time with her friends and family.

Find Erica on:

https://sites.google.com/view/marielapres/home?authuser=1

Facebook: "Marie LaPres"

e-mail~ericamarie84@gmail.com

GoodReads: Marie LaPres

Instagram: marielapres

The Turner Daughter Series	
Though War Shall Rise Against Me	The war between the states has finally come and the civilians of Gettysburg hope the battles will stay as far away from them as possible. But the war will touch them all more than they can imagine. Four friends, old and new, will find themselves looking to God and each other to get them through.
Be Strong and Steadfast	Kate, America Joan, and sisters Belle and Elizabeth enjoy their lives in the safe, "finished" town of Fredericksburg, Virginia. Then, the Civil War breaks out and their lives will never be the same. Will the Civil War affect the women and their town? Will they lose faith, or always remain 'Strong and Steadfast'?
Plans for a Future of Hope	The citizens of Vicksburg never wanted secession, much less a war, but when Mississippi secedes from the United States, they throw their support behind the Confederacy. They hope the battles will stay far away from their bustling trade center, but they realize the importance of their town, perfectly situated atop a hill at a bend on the mighty Mississippi River. Then the siege comes…
Wherever You Go A Prequel Novella	As the United States are being pulled apart, one Southern belle must decide between love and comfort. Will Augusta Byron let her family down and risk social rejection from friends? Or will the problems facing the nation keep her from the man she is falling in love with?
Stand-Alone Novel	
Wisdom and Humility	Newcomers to the Black Hills in South Dakota bring romance and heartbreak to several of the local women. Then there is the handsome, yet frustratingly pretentious Lucas Callahan who seems to be at the heart of all the strife. As Luke and Ellie are continually thrown together in different scenarios, their feelings for one another seem to be on a turbulent journey. Neither one can decide how they feel for the other. When several misfortunes come to the Bennet family, will they be able to work through them or will they lose their reputations as well as their ranch? Will both Luke and Ellie be able to find the wisdom they need to make some tough decisions?
Middle Grade Novel	

Whom Shall I Fear? Sammy's Struggle	Twelve-year-old Samuel Wade's life has never been easy, but the coming of the American Civil War makes it even more difficult. Then the war comes to his hometown of Gettysburg and he must make quick decisions that could mean life or death.
The Key to Mackinac Series: Young Adult Novels	
Beyond the Fort	16-year-old Christine Belanger has always loved learning about the past, but she may get more history than she bargained for when she finds herself at Colonial Michilimackinac in the year 1775. While there, Christine helps uncover a plot to eradicate all the French settlers. It falls to Christine and her new friend Henri to save the French settlers, and possibly change the course of history.
Beyond the Island	When Rafael Lafontaine decides to go back in time, he doesn't count on Sadie Morrison following him and they quickly realize that nothing is as it should be. Will they be able to thwart his objectives without changing history? Will they be able to get back home or do they even want to return?